Merry Christmas

Treasury of Stories and Songs

Cover Illustration by
Scott Gustafson

 publications international, ltd.

ISBN: 0-7853-7033-1

CONTENTS

The First Christmas 7

Yes, Virginia, There Is a Santa Claus 27

The Meaning of Christmas 31

The Christmas Miracle 43

A Christmas Carol 65

Christmas Pageant 85

Waiting for Santa 103

Christmas Gifts 121

The Night Before Christmas 141

The Tailor's Apprentices 161

Jingle Bells 177

The Nutcracker 195

Christmas Socks 217

The Perfect Tree 229

The Gift of the Magi 247

God Rest Ye Merry Gentlemen 266

Here We Come A-Caroling 268

O Christmas Tree 270

O Little Town of Bethlehem 272

While Shepherds Watched Their Flocks 274

O Come All Ye Faithful 276

Joy to the World 278

Hark! The Herald Angels Sing 280

What Child Is This 282

Away in a Manger 284

Silent Night 286

The First Noel 288

We Three Kings 290

The Twelve Days of Christmas. 292

Jolly Old St. Nicholas 296

Up on the Housetop 298

Jingle Bells. 300

Dance of the Sugar Plum Fairy 302

Toyland 304

Deck the Halls 306

I Saw Three Ships 308

O Holy Night 310

We Wish You a Merry Christmas 314

Angels We Have Heard on High 316

It Came Upon a Midnight Clear 318

THE FIRST CHRISTMAS

Written by Sarah Toast

Illustrated by Mike Jaroszko

God had promised to send his son to earth to be the world's Savior. When the time was right, God sent the angel Gabriel to Nazareth. There a young maiden named Mary lived. Mary was engaged to wed Joseph, a carpenter.

The angel appeared to Mary and said, "Rejoice! The Lord is with you. Do not be afraid, Mary. God has greatly blessed you. You are going to have a baby, and you will name him Jesus. He will be the Son of God. His kingdom will never end."

Joseph was worried about Mary having a baby that was not his. Then the angel Gabriel appeared to Joseph in a dream. He told Joseph about Mary's holy child. Joseph understood. He wed Mary and took care of her.

Some months later, Rome's emperor announced that everyone in the land had to be counted. Men had to return to their hometown. There they would tell their name and what land they owned.

Joseph belonged to the family line of David. King David's birthplace was Bethlehem. So it was that Joseph left Nazareth, in Galilee, and set out for the distant town of Bethlehem, in Judea.

Joseph's young wife, Mary, went with him. She was nearing the time when she would give birth.

It was a long and difficult journey. Even though Mary rode the donkey while Joseph walked, she was weary. Her spirits lifted when they came to fields where sheep were grazing. Then the little town of Bethlehem came into view.

Night was falling when Joseph and Mary arrived in Bethlehem. Cattle were being led to the stables outside the town. The lamps were lit in the houses and inns.

Mary and Joseph knocked on the door of the first inn and waited. After what seemed like a long time, the innkeeper came to the door with his lantern.

The innkeeper told Joseph that he had no rooms left. Joseph and Mary tried several inns, but none of them had any rooms because so many people were staying in Bethlehem.

Finally one innkeeper noticed that Mary was heavy with child. The innkeeper told Joseph and Mary that they could spend the night in his stable with the animals.

That night in the stable, Mary gave birth to her baby, the Son of God. Mary wrapped the babe in light swaddling cloths and laid him in a manger. Mary and Joseph named the baby Jesus.

The manger was filled with soft, clean hay, intended to feed the cattle. This was the first bed for the infant Jesus.

Mary rested near the manger while her newborn son slept peacefully. Joseph sat quietly beside her. The gentle animals in the stable crowded near the infant. Their sweet breath warmed the family.

Outside in the dark night sky, a bright new star appeared in the east. This was a very special star and it shone like no other star in the sky. It has come to be known as the Star of Bethlehem.

In the fields outside the town, shepherds were keeping watch over their sheep through the night.

Suddenly there was a great light, and an angel of the Lord appeared before them. The shepherds were very much afraid.

The angel spoke to the shepherds, saying, "Fear not, for I bring you wonderful news. It will bring great joy to all the world. For there is born to you this night in Bethlehem a savior, who is Christ the Lord. And this is how you will know him: You will find a baby wrapped in swaddling cloths, lying in a manger."

Then all at once many angels appeared in the sky.

The angels sang praises: "Glory to God in the highest, and on earth peace and goodwill toward all people."

The shepherds said to one another, "Let us go to this baby that God's angels have told us about."

The shepherds hurried to Bethlehem through the bright, starlit night. Soon they found Mary and Joseph resting in the stable, and the baby Jesus wrapped in swaddling cloths asleep in the manger. Back at their fields, they told everyone that they had seen the Savior. All who heard were very amazed!

In a land far to the east, there lived three wise men, Gaspar, Melchior, and Balthasar.

On the night of Jesus' birth, the Wise Men saw a bright new star in the heavens. They knew the star was a sign that the Savior had been born. They learned that Bethlehem was the birthplace.

They decided they must go worship the newborn King. They gathered gifts of gold, frankincense, and myrrh and set off on their long journey.

The three Wise Men traveled the long road to Bethlehem by camel caravan with their gifts for Baby Jesus. To their great joy and wonder, the same bright star that they had seen first in the east went ahead of them. Its light guided them on their long journey. The star's ever-present glow led them over the hills and across valleys.

The Wise Men followed the star westward until they reached Bethlehem. Then the Star of Bethlehem seemed to stand still. It streamed its light down on a small stable. The Wise Men knew that this must be where the infant Jesus lay. They approached the stable.

It had been a long journey, but the Wise Men had finally reached their destination. They came to the place the star was shining on. Inside the stable, they saw the baby with his mother, Mary. Gazing on the child, the Wise Men fell to their knees and worshiped the infant.

Then they opened the treasures they had brought from the east. They presented the infant Jesus with the rare gifts of gold, frankincense, and myrrh. Then they thanked God for showing them the way.

Soon others came from all over the land to worship the newborn Son of God. They knew that he was a very wonderful child and that the day he was born would always be remembered as a very special day throughout time.

Mary looked lovingly at her child. She thought about how the Lord had blessed her. In her heart, she praised the Lord, and her spirit rejoiced.

From then on, the day that Baby Jesus was born would be known as Christmas Day and the world would celebrate!

YES, VIRGINIA, THERE IS A SANTA CLAUS

Illustrated by Wayne Parmenter

In 1897, eight-year-old Virginia O'Hanlon asked the question, "Is there a Santa Claus?" She wrote a letter to the editor of *The New York Sun* requesting an honest reply.

This is what her letter said:

Dear Editor:

I am eight years old. Some of my little friends say there is no Santa Claus. Papa says, "If you see it in The Sun it's so."

Please tell me the truth, is there a Santa Claus?

Virginia O'Hanlon
115 West 95th Street

Francis P. Church was an editor for *The Sun*. He received little Virginia's letter and wrote the following reply. It was printed in the September 21, 1897 edition of *The New York Sun*.

Virginia, your little friends are wrong. They have been affected by the skepticism of a skeptical age. They do not believe except they see. They think that nothing can be which is not comprehensible by their little minds. All minds, Virginia, whether they be men's or children's, are little. In this great universe of ours man is a mere insect, an ant, in his intellect, as compared with the boundless world about him, as measured by the intelligence capable of grasping the whole of truth and knowledge.

Yes, Virginia, there is a Santa Claus. He exists as certainly as love and generosity and devotion exist, and you know that they abound and give to your life its highest beauty and joy. Alas, how dreary would be the world if there were no Santa Claus! It would be as dreary as if there were no Virginias.

There would be no childlike faith then, no poetry, no romance to make tolerable this existence. We should have no enjoyment, except in sense and sight. The eternal light with which childhood fills the world would be extinguished.

Not believe in Santa Claus! You might as well not believe in fairies! You might get your papa to hire men to watch in all the chimneys on Christmas Eve to catch Santa Claus coming down, but what would that prove? Nobody sees Santa Claus.

The most real things in the world are those that neither children nor men can see. Did you ever see fairies dancing on the lawn? Of course not, but that's no proof that they are not there. Nobody can conceive or imagine all of the wonders there are unseen and unseeable in the world.

You tear apart a baby's rattle and see what makes the noise inside, but there is a veil covering the unseen world which not the strongest man, nor the united strength of all the strongest men that ever lived, could tear apart. Only faith, fancy, poetry, love, romance can push aside that curtain and view and picture the supernal beauty and glory beyond. Is it all real? Ah, Virginia, in this world there is nothing else real and abiding.

No Santa Claus! Thank God he lives, and lives forever. A thousand years from now, Virginia, he will continue to make glad the heart of childhood.

THE MEANING OF CHRISTMAS

Written by Lisa Harkrader

Illustrated by Deborah Colvin Borgo

Santa looked at the line of children waiting to see him. "Christmas means so much to the kids," he said.

One by one the children sat on Santa's lap. One by one they told Santa what they wanted for Christmas. Each child had a longer list than the child before. Santa listened as the children asked for more and more and bigger and bigger presents.

"Oh, dear!" thought Santa. "Have I been too busy making lists and building toys? Did I let the kids forget the true meaning of Christmas?"

Santa began asking each child, "What do you think Christmas is about?"

"Presents, of course," said Jeff.

"Vacation from school," said Amanda.

"Cookies," said Ross, "with frosting."

Nate was last in line. He scrambled onto Santa's lap. Santa looked at the long, long list that Nate had in his hand and sighed.

Nate smoothed out his list and began reading.

"First of all," said Nate, "I need garden tools. And there's a very good reason why."

Santa barely listened to Nate as he read his list. He was too sad and too worried. He was sad the kids didn't remember the meaning of Christmas. He was worried that he had been too busy to help them remember. He heard Nate say something about a music box, a barbecue grill, and dog biscuits.

Santa sat up straight. "Dog biscuits?"

"Yes," said Nate. "The flavored kind."

Santa shook his head. "If that's what you want." He gave Nate a candy cane and sent him on his way. Santa didn't ask Nate why he wanted dog biscuits. He didn't ask Nate what he thought Christmas really meant either.

Christmas Eve arrived, and Santa was running late. His bag was so heavy it bogged down the sleigh. It was so bulky Santa could barely get it down the chimneys.

"It's the toys," Santa told Blitzen. "There are more toys this year than ever before."

By the time Santa reached Nate's house, it was almost midnight. Nate was already fast asleep.

"It's almost Christmas Day," Santa told Blitzen, "and I haven't found anybody who knows what Christmas is all about."

The sleigh landed on Nate's roof. Santa checked to make sure all of Nate's gifts were in his bag. "Nate asked for some peculiar gifts this year," he said. "Garden tools, a music box, a barbecue grill, and dog biscuits."

Santa heaved his bulging bag over his shoulder. "I've really let the kids down," he told Blitzen. "They think Christmas is what I carry in this bag. It's all my fault."

Blitzen snorted and stamped his hoof on the snow-covered roof.

"Snort all you like. It's true," Santa said.

"Wish me luck," Santa said. "You know what happened at the Murphy house."

Santa grabbed his bag firmly, climbed into the chimney, and slid down. Halfway to the bottom, Santa's bulging bag skidded to a stop. Santa and the toys were stuck.

"Oh dear," said Santa. "I was afraid of this."

Santa tugged on the bag. It slid free. Santa landed with a thud in the fireplace.

"Just like the Murphy house," he mumbled as he brushed soot off his jacket.

Santa set about his business, leaving gifts for Nate and his family. He pulled the first gift from his bag.

"I can't imagine what Nate wants with garden tools. Still, it's what he asked for." Santa consulted his list. "Oh my." Santa blinked. "Nate doesn't want these tools for himself. They're for his mother."

Santa scratched his head. He thought back to the day Nate had come to sit on his lap. He tried to remember what Nate had said. "Nate told me his mother loves her garden, but her old tools are rusty. Ho-ho-ho! I should have paid closer attention."

Santa studied his list even closer.

"The music box is for his sister, and the barbecue grill is for his dad. Nate wanted to make sure his family got exactly what they wanted. He even remembered dog biscuits for his dog. Well, I won't let them down."

Santa bounded about the room, leaving gifts and filling stockings. When he reached Nate's stocking, he found something already inside. It was a small wrapped package with a little tag and a green bow. The tag said, "To Santa."

Santa opened the gift. It was a pair of earmuffs.
Underneath was a note:

Dear Santa,

You forgot to ask me what Christmas is all about. Jeff said
Christmas is about presents, and he's right. I make my family
happy when I give them a gift that
they really want.

Amanda said Christmas is about vacation, and she's right, too. During Christmas break my family has time to decorate our tree and bake cookies. That means Ross was right, too. Christmas is about cookies.

But mostly I think Christmas is about believing in things you love, even when they're hard to see. Like you.

Love,

Nate

P.S. I hope you like the earmuffs. I don't want you to get sick. Christmas wouldn't be Christmas without you.

Santa read the letter twice. "Nate's right," he said. "Christmas is about believing in the things you love. The kids didn't forget that, but I did. I stopped believing in the kids."

As Santa turned to leave, he saw the time on the mantel clock. Midnight had passed. It was now officially Christmas Day.

"Well, it's Christmas and I finally found somebody who remembers the true meaning of Christmas," Santa said, donning his earmuffs. "Little Nate and me, too."

Santa patted his new earmuffs and put a little extra something in Nate's stocking. It turned out that he didn't let the children down after all.

THE CHRISTMAS MIRACLE

Written by Pegeen Hopkins

Illustrated by Linda Graves

Once upon a time there lived a poor Dutch baker. He never had enough money to buy food. Each winter, the baker's problems got worse. When the temperature fell, people stayed home and didn't buy bread.

One December night, the wind was blowing strong and not a single person had come in that day. "What will I do?" the baker muttered. It was getting late, so he locked the bakery door. The baker walked off into the cold, gray afternoon.

Every day the baker skated along an icy canal to get to the bakery. "I will carry the leftover bread home to my wife," he thought. He knew she would be disappointed with the sales of the bakery, but she would take the bread and make the best of it.

He walked slowly to the frozen canal, with his teeth chattering the whole way. When he got to the canal, the baker could see the farmer coming toward him.

The farmer didn't have much luck at the market, either. He had hoped to sell the apples from his tiny orchard. But by the end of the day he had sold only ten. He had to bring his sackful of apples home so they wouldn't go bad in the frost. This made him sad. He needed guilders, small Dutch coins, to buy medicine for his daughter who was very sick.

The two men greeted each other quietly and began skating together. Their skates soon fell into a rhythm.

Before long, another man appeared on the canal. As he skated toward the baker and the farmer, he thought about his long day.

The new skater was a talented weaver on his way home from the marketplace, too. He made warm blankets and pretty coats. But no one could buy the weaver's goods. Most people in the small Dutch town made do with what they had. They rarely bought anything new.

The weaver had wanted to make enough to buy his old father the lemon tea he liked so much. But all the weaver had was blankets. Like the other two men, he had no money. "It will be wonderful to get out of this chill," said the weaver, trying to start some cheerful conversation.

The other two men just nodded their heads in agreement. Their thick scarves and the biting wind made it hard to talk to one another. They continued along the canal in silence.

A cold, sharp blast of wind hit the men as they skated. So they lowered their heads to protect themselves from the cold. They listened to the wind blowing through the trees on the side of the canal. The whining of the wind seemed to get louder and louder. It became so strong that it sounded like a baby crying.

The farmer saw an old, deserted stable in the distance. He had fond memories of playing there when he was a boy. But that was many years ago. Now the stable was in ruins.

The farmer realized that the crying sound was not the wind. It was coming from inside the stable. "That can't be," he thought out loud. "No one has been in that stable for years."

"That sounds like a child," said the baker.

Without another word, the three men stepped off the ice and into the snow. As they reached the door, they could hear the baby's cries beginning to soften. Soon they heard the gentle sound of a mother's voice singing a soulful lullaby.

The men pushed the door aside and looked in. They could not believe their eyes. A young woman sat on the floor, holding a baby boy in her arms. She stopped singing as she looked up at the men. Then she smiled.

It had been the baby making the noise, not the wind. A man sat next to them on a crate. He held his head in his hands, looking very sad.

"What are you doing here?" asked the baker. "This is no place for a family. It is much too cold. You can't stay here."

"We are traveling through Amsterdam on our way to visit relatives," the man replied. "It got so cold and dark we had to find shelter."

The farmer turned to look at the young woman and the baby, who was now fast asleep. "What will you eat?" the farmer asked. When he looked at the peaceful boy, he immediately thought of his sick daughter at home. She had looked so fragile and tiny when he left her that morning.

"We have nothing," replied the young man. He started raking the hay together to make a bed.

"Here," the baker exclaimed suddenly, "take these loaves of bread. It's not much. But you need it more than I do."

One by one, the men took their sacks and emptied them in front of the woman and child. They stacked the bread, apples, and blankets in neat piles on the floor. The family looked at the men in awe.

"My prayers have been answered," cried the woman. "Our son was so hungry and cold. We will not forget your kindness. But we can never repay you. We are very poor."

"We understand," replied the men.

During the short time the men were in the stable, the wind had died down. A light snow began to fall. Each man felt a warm feeling inside. Their thoughts and their bags did not weigh them down anymore. They left the barn and skated down the canal. Each man smiled, because they knew they would be home soon.

"Maybe our luck will be better tomorrow at the marketplace," said the baker. But the men's luck would change sooner than tomorrow.

As they skated toward home, the men felt the sacks on their backs getting heavier, as if they were filling up.

"The snow must be falling hard," each man thought. "I can feel it falling in my bag."

When the baker reached his house and left the others, they saw that his bag was fat and bulging. "Merry Christmas," he said to his new friends. The farmer and the weaver waved back at him as he walked toward his house.

Then the baker removed his skates and trudged through the heavy snow. When he arrived home, he opened his front door. Only then did he see that his bag was bulging, but not with snow, as he had thought. The bag was bursting with gold coins and food of all sorts! There was even a silk scarf for his wife and toys for the children.

"My, the market must have been very busy today," said the baker's wife. "How can we afford all of these wonderful gifts?"

The baker could not explain the wonderful gifts. He just shook his head and said, "I guess we deserve them, dear."

That night the baker and his family had the best dinner ever.

When it was time for bed, the baker gathered the children in front of the fire and told them about the amazing story of the family in the old barn.

After he put his family to bed with full bellies, the baker sat up and looked out the window. At that moment, the baker knew that when his friends got home they had found their bags filled with gifts, too.

And they did. When the farmer reached his house, he turned to the weaver and said, "I hope we will meet on the canal again."

"Merry Christmas," said the weaver.

The farmer went into his house. Then he realized why his bag felt so full. It held many guilders and enough medicine to cure his sick daughter!

The weaver found the same fortune upon his return home. His bag was full of the lemon tea his father loved so much!

For their kindness, the baker, the weaver, and the farmer had found more than good luck. They had found a miracle.

A CHRISTMAS CAROL

Adapted by Lisa Harkrader

Illustrated by Lydia Halverson

Ebenezer Scrooge hunched over his account books. Scrooge's clerk, Bob Crachit, huddled at his own desk. The front door burst open, and a blast of December air whipped through the room.

"Merry Christmas, Uncle!" said Scrooge's nephew.

"Christmas," muttered Scrooge. "Bah! Humbug!"

"You can't mean that, Uncle," said his nephew. "Why don't you close early today?"

"And become like other Christmas fools, buying gifts I can't afford?" said Scrooge. "No, thank you."

"Suit yourself," said his nephew. "But I hope you'll at least stop by for Christmas dinner tomorrow."

When his nephew opened the door, another gust of wind burst into the office. With it came the sound of carolers singing.

Scrooge banged his window open. "You!" he shouted at the carolers.

One of the carolers stopped singing and stared up at Scrooge.

"Find another street corner," Scrooge snarled. He banged the window shut.

"Sir?" said Bob Crachit, tapping on Scrooge's door. "I've filed the paperwork."

"Fine," said Scrooge. "You may leave."

"Mr. Scrooge?" said Crachit. "Tomorrow is Christmas, a day to spend with family."

"Christmas? Bah!" Scrooge shook his head. "Fine. Take tomorrow off, but be here early the next day."

Crachit was very happy as he rushed out the door.

"Fool," Scrooge scowled.

Darkness fell, and Scrooge closed the last account book. It was time to go home.

As he locked the door, he glanced at the sign above. It read: THE FIRM OF SCROOGE AND MARLEY.

"Jacob Marley," said Scrooge. "A man who knew the value of a day's work. Too bad he's gone."

Scrooge trudged home, climbed the steps to his bedroom, and fell asleep.

CLANK! "What was that?" said Scrooge. He listened carefully but heard nothing. "Perhaps I'm dreaming," he muttered.

CLANK! Scrooge sat up straight in his bed.

"No, it isn't a dream," said a voice that echoed through Scrooge's bedroom. A man, pale and ghostly, drifted into the room.

Scrooge stared at him. "Marley? Jacob Marley?"

"How can that be? You're . . ."

"Dead," the ghost said. "And paying for my sins."

Scrooge frowned. "But you were a fine businessman."

"Business? Hah!" said Marley's ghost as he shivered. "I never learned the value of love and charity. Now I wander the earth, unable to find peace."

"I don't understand, Jacob," Scrooge whispered.

"The same fate awaits you," the ghost said, "unless you change your ways. Three spirits will visit you. The first will arrive when the clock strikes one."

The ghost silently vanished, and Scrooge pulled the covers over his head.

BONG! The clock struck one. "Ebenezer Scrooge?"

Scrooge peeked out at a woman standing beside his bed. "Who are you?" whispered Scrooge.

"I am the Ghost of Christmas Past," said the ghost as she motioned toward the door.

Scrooge followed the ghost. The room began to dissolve, and soon he was staring into the window of another room.

"This house," said Scrooge. "It seems familiar. Why, it's the house I grew up in."

"Yes." The ghost nodded. "And the boy? Is he familiar, too?"

Scrooge peered through the window. A small boy sat alone in the corner, reading a book. Scrooge's eyes grew wide. "It's me as a child! But why is he sitting all by himself?" Scrooge stared at the boy.

"Your parents are at work," said the ghost. Scrooge studied the boy. He looked well-dressed, but his eyes were very sad. "We have many places to visit," said the ghost. "Come." The small, dark house faded away, and in its place stood a bright office filled with workers. "I know this office!" said Scrooge.

Scrooge pointed to a man carrying a platter of roast beef into the office. "That's Mr. Fezziwig," he said. Mrs. Fezziwig followed with a tray of pastries.

"Stop your work," Mr. Fezziwig told the office clerks. "It's Christmas Eve!"

A fiddler began playing, and Mr. and Mrs. Fezziwig danced a lively jig around the office.

The Ghost of Christmas Past glanced at Scrooge. "This certainly isn't the firm of Scrooge and Marley, is it? Do you recognize the clerk in the corner?"

Scrooge stared at the young man. "It's me," he said. The young Scrooge laughed and clapped to the music. His eyes were bright, so very different from Scrooge's own clerk, Bob Crachit, who had huddled in the cold the night before.

"I hope this party never ends," young Scrooge called out. "Let's stay and dance forever!"

Old Scrooge thought about Crachit, who had run from the office on Christmas Eve. "Crachit couldn't wait to get away from me," he said.

The music faded. Fezziwig's office dissolved into darkness.

"We have one more stop," said the ghost. "Our time is running out."

The ghost waved her arms, and Scrooge saw his younger self again, sitting in a garden beside a lovely young woman.

The woman's eyes filled with tears as she said, "I can't marry you, Ebenezer. There's something you love more than me."

"Nonsense," said the young Ebenezer.

The woman dabbed her eyes with her handkerchief. "You love money. You love it more than anything." The woman ran from the garden.

Old Scrooge and the ghost followed her. Scrooge could see she was now a few years older. She was in a parlor that had been decorated for Christmas. Children laughed and played at her feet. A little girl threw her arms around her.

"You could have made her happy," the ghost said.

"Take me home!" Scrooge said. "I can't bear to see this.

BONG!

BONG!

The clock struck two. Scrooge was back in his own bed. "Thank goodness," he said. "It was a dream."

"No, Ebenezer. It wasn't a dream." A man stared down at Scrooge. "I am the Ghost of Christmas Present," he said. "I have much to show you. Grab onto my robe." Scrooge touched the spirit's robe. Then the bedroom vanished, and Scrooge found himself on a busy street. The dark of night was gone.

Men and women bustled along the sidewalks. Children laughed and skipped at their sides.

"Everyone looks so happy," grumbled Scrooge.

"Of course they do," said the ghost. "It's Christmas."

Scrooge shook his head. "You mean they all woke up happy, simply because it is December 25?"

The ghost smiled. "Yes. Today they can forget their troubles and simply enjoy their families. When was the last time you stopped and enjoyed the moment? Try it now. Close your eyes."

Scrooge frowned and closed his eyes. The aroma of freshly baked bread mingled in the crisp morning air. Horses clip-clopped over the cobblestone street. An icy snowflake tickled his tongue, and his mouth stretched into a wide smile.

The ghost led Scrooge down the street and into a tiny house. Beside a small Christmas tree, a man was playing with his children. The man looked up. He was Scrooge's clerk, Bob Crachit.

"Crachit!" Scrooge frowned. "He lives here?"

The ghost nodded. "It's all he can afford."

Mrs. Crachit carried a small turkey into the room. She smiled as she carried the platter to the table.

The older children giggled and raced to the table.

"Their clothes are rags," said Scrooge, "and their turkey is nothing but bones."

Bob Crachit lifted the youngest boy from a chair in the corner and carried him to the table. The boy was pale and thin and carried a crutch. His name was Tiny Tim.

Tiny Tim raised his cup of water and smiled. "Merry Christmas!" he said. "God bless us every one."

"What is wrong with that child?" Scrooge asked.

"Come," said the ghost, and he turned to leave.

"Wait," Scrooge said. "Their child is hurt, their turkey is all bones. Tell me why they are so happy."

BONG! BONG! BONG! Scrooge blinked. He was in his own bed again. The Ghost of Christmas Present was gone.

But as Scrooge sat up, another ghost floated into the room. "Who are you?" he asked. "You must be the Ghost of Christmas Yet to Come."

The phantom gestured toward the door. Scrooge followed him to the countinghouse. Three men stood out front. The ghost led Scrooge closer.

"Poor old Scrooge," said one. "They say he's very sick."

"If I know Ebenezer," said another man, "he'll work during his own funeral."

"It is bad news, though," said the third man. "If Scrooge closes down, I'll have to find another countinghouse."

Scrooge turned to the ghost. "But I'm not closing down."

The phantom turned. Scrooge followed him to a tiny room with faded walls. "But this is Crachit's house," Scrooge said. "I've already seen them."

The spirit shook his head and led Scrooge into a bedroom. Mr. Crachit held Tiny Tim's hand.

"What's wrong with them?" asked Scrooge.

Mrs. Crachit came in. Scrooge watched Tiny Tim. His face was drawn and pale.

"We can't go on without Tiny Tim," said Mrs. Crachit.

"Without Tiny Tim?" Scrooge gasped. "But that can't be. Is he dying?"

The ghost nodded and turned toward the door.

"No!" cried Scrooge.
"We must help him!"
The Crachit's house
faded away. Scrooge found
himself outside. He glanced
around. A gravel path led through
rows of granite stones.

"This is a cemetery," said Scrooge.
"Oh, no. Not Tiny Tim. Is it too late?"

The ghost pointed at a new grave.
Engraved on a simple stone were two
words: EBENEZER SCROOGE.

Scrooge stared. "Mine?" he whispered.
"The grave is mine." Scrooge closed his
eyes. He fell to his knees.

"Give me another chance," cried Scrooge.

He opened his eyes. He was in his own room. From his open window, he spotted a boy on the street. "You there!" he shouted. "What day is this?"

"It's Christmas, sir," the boy said.

"Good! Please, do me a favor." Scrooge pulled out a bag of money. He tossed some coins to the boy.

"There's a big, juicy turkey in the butcher shop. Buy it and deliver it to Bob Crachit's house."

The boy held up the coins. "Sir, this is twice the cost of the turkey."

Scrooge laughed. "Keep the rest for your trouble."

The boy grinned. "Yes, sir!" He scurried away.

Scrooge dressed in his finest clothes, planted his top hat on his head, and headed to his nephew's house.

Everything looked very familiar to Scrooge. "It's just like before," he said.

He tipped his hat to a group of carolers. "Merry Christmas," said Scrooge.

"Merry Christmas to you," said the carolers.

Scrooge's nephew was surprised to see him. "Uncle!" he cried. "Did you change your mind about dinner?"

"Yes," said Scrooge. "If you will have me."

"We'd be delighted to have you!" said his nephew.

After dinner, Scrooge said, "Thank you. I hate to leave, but I have another stop to make."

He hurried down the street to Bob Crachit's house. From that day on, each time he sat down to a meal, Scrooge would raise his glass in a toast. "God bless us," he would say. "God bless us every one."

CHRISTMAS PAGEANT

Written by Mary Rowitz

Illustrated by Kathleen O'Malley

It is the first night of the Christmas pageant. Nervous children are running here and there. They are getting ready to play the parts of Mary, Joseph, the shepherds, and the three Wise Men. They will tell the story of the birth of Jesus.

Parents file into the church. Jimmy, who is dressed up in his special shepherd's costume, grips his father's hand tightly. He is very nervous. He worries that he will forget some of his lines. But his father soon makes him feel better.

"Jimmy, if you forget what you are supposed to say, think about the meaning of the story," Jimmy's father says. "That should help you think of what line comes next." Jimmy lets go of his father's hand and hurries to the stage.

Jimmy watches his friends Greg and Sarah go on stage. They will be playing Joseph and Mary at the pageant. At rehearsals, Greg and Sarah had always giggled when they said their lines. But now, they both look very serious. Sarah carries a doll that is supposed to be the Baby Jesus.

On stage, Greg notices that the boy playing the innkeeper has buttoned up his shirt wrong! Greg thinks this is very funny. But he clears his throat and says his lines, without even a tiny giggle. "May we have a place to stay?" he asks.

"I have no room in my inn," says the innkeeper. "But you may stay in my stable."

Off stage, Greg and Sarah burst out laughing. Jimmy giggles, too.

Now it's Jimmy's turn on stage. He walks out from behind the curtain. There are so many faces in the audience! Jimmy tries not to look at them. Instead he looks at his feet. Now he does not feel so nervous.

Jimmy bends down to feed a lamb, but he cannot remember his lines! He thinks about the meaning of the story, like his father told him. He takes a deep breath and remembers his lines.

"Christ the Savior is born today," Jimmy says. "Let's praise the Baby Jesus."

Jimmy looks at the audience. The faces are all smiling! Jimmy smiles, bows, and looks around for his father. His father gives him a wink. Jimmy hurries off the stage.

Jimmy stands backstage now. He is bouncing with excitement. He delivered his first set of lines without a problem. His father's trick really worked. Now his friend Tina takes the stage. She begins by singing a Christmas song.

With her big smile and bright sparkling eyes, Tina looks exactly like an angel should, Jimmy thinks to himself.

As Tina steps across the stage, her right shoe slips off and lands at the edge of the stage! But she keeps singing. Tina takes off her other shoe and sits down. Then she sings another Christmas tune.

Jimmy looks at Tina on stage and thinks that angels should not wear shoes anyway. "They must get in the way when they are flying," thinks Jimmy.

Now it is time for Jimmy's next scene. When Rob, the other shepherd, joins him on stage, Jimmy sees that he is very nervous. Jimmy remembers his father and winks at Rob. He says, "Just do what I do, and you'll be fine."

Rob smiles at his friend. "Okay," he says. "I'll just follow you."

Jimmy kneels. So does Rob.

Jimmy bows his head. Rob bows his head, too.

"Baby Jesus," Jimmy says, "you will have many special friends in your life."

Then Rob remembers his line. "They will be thankful to be your friend," he says.

Rob is thankful Jimmy is his friend. "Thank you for helping me," he whispers to Jimmy.

As Jimmy walks off stage, the three Wise Men, played by Matt, Andy, and Sean, are walking on. The night before, Jimmy helped them pick out gifts for the Baby Jesus.

First comes Matt. He brought some of his best rocks from his rock collection. He carries them in a pretty, colorful box. He leads the way wearing a red robe and a big smile.

Next comes Andy, who put his favorite jelly beans in a jar. He ate a few backstage, but there are still plenty left.

Last comes Sean, who brought his pet mouse. The little mouse squeaks as the boys walk up the aisle. Sean just hopes no one opens the box on stage! And he hopes the Baby Jesus likes his gift.

Now Jimmy and the other children gather on stage. A bright spotlight shines down on the baby. The shepherds and Wise Men gather around him. The three Wise Men kneel down and offer their gifts to little Jesus.

Jimmy and Rob are no longer so nervous. They think about how shepherds should behave. John and Sarah no longer feel like giggling. They think about how Mary and Joseph would have felt. Sean forgets about his pet mouse in his box. He pretends to have myrrh in his box now.

The children close their eyes and pretend that they are in Bethlehem on the day Jesus is born. Soon they forget that their parents are watching them. They bow their heads and pray to the Baby Jesus.

Jimmy watches as Sarah holds the Baby Jesus. She is playing the part of Mary. Jimmy hopes she does not giggle during this last scene.

Jimmy has nothing to worry about. Sarah holds the baby tightly. Then she looks at the baby and speaks just as a mother would.

"I love you very much," she says. "You are my special baby. As you grow up, I want you to laugh and have fun. But just remember that there are times to be serious, too."

Everyone thinks Sarah has chosen the perfect words to say. Soon the church is filled with applause. All the parents stand up and clap for their children. The children smile and take a bow. They are very proud of themselves.

Jimmy's father is very proud of him, too. He runs to greet Jimmy after the play is over. "You did a wonderful job!" he says.

Sarah, Jimmy, and the rest of the children have managed to capture the true meaning of Christmas with their play. Their performance has made this the most wonderful Christmas pageant the town has ever seen!

WAITING FOR SANTA

Written by Pegeen Hopkins

Illustrated by Kathleen O'Malley

Sally climbs the stairs and gets ready for bed. She brushes her teeth and changes into her favorite nightgown. "Grandma, when will Santa be here?" little Sally asks as she crawls into the big bed.

It is Christmas Eve. Everyone knows that on Christmas Eve, each minute is as long as a day. And it is very difficult to fall asleep, too.

"Santa will be here before you know it," Grandma says. "Let me tell you a story while we wait. When I was your age, I knew a young girl just like you. She looked very much like you, too. This little girl's name was Lucy. She waited for Santa, too. As she helped her family decorate the house for Christmas, she asked her mother if Santa really lived on the North Pole, or right here in town."

"When the decorations were up, Lucy ran to find her grandfather. Surely he knew about Santa. He looked as old as Saint Nick, and he seemed to know everything. He had a bushy white beard, rosy cheeks, and when he laughed, his big round belly shook just like jelly. But his voice was the greatest. It was so deep, it rang out like a church bell.

"'Grandie, when will Santa get here?' Lucy asked. 'I've been waiting all day.'

"'That's just it,' her grandfather said. 'Santa only comes when you least expect him. That's the way all great things arrive.'

"'Well, I don't think I can wait any longer,' said Lucy. 'I wish he would come right now.'

"'You must be patient,' her grandfather said."

"Was he right?" Sally asks Grandma. "Does Santa really come when you least expect him?"

"You'll see," Grandma answers. "Lucy joined her mother in the bedroom where they put on their best clothes. They were getting all dressed up for their family Christmas party."

"'Mama,' Lucy said, 'Grandie knows so much. Don't you think he looks just like Santa? And Santa IS supposed to know everything. Grandie knows in a snap if I've been bad, even if he has been out. I think he might be Santa Claus.'

"Lucy's mother sighed. 'He is a special man,' she said, 'but do you really think he could be THE Santa Claus? Being Santa Claus is a very important job. I'm not sure your grandfather has time.'"

"Later that afternoon, Lucy and her family sat around the blazing fire to sing Christmas carols. The singing stopped short when a loud thud came from the chimney.

"'What was that?' Lucy asked. 'I hear Santa! He's coming right now!' She ran out to the yard. But when she looked up on the roof, the roof was empty. Lucy trudged back inside.

"'That wasn't Santa at all,' Lucy said to her grandfather.

"'Do you think,' said Lucy's grandfather, 'that Santa would come down a chimney filled with smoke and fire?'

"'You're right,' she replied. 'I'll have to wait for the fire to burn out.'"

"When the guests finally arrived and the party began, Lucy wondered how the other guests could be so patient. Weren't they thinking about Santa's arrival, too?

"'It's getting late, Grandie,' said Lucy. 'Maybe Santa is stuck in an ice storm and can't make it. Or one of his reindeer is sick and can't fly. Or maybe the elves forgot to make the toys.'

"'Remember, my dear, you have to have faith,' said her grandfather. 'Be patient. There is no use in trying to figure him out. I think he wants to keep his comings and goings a secret. Otherwise, you would not be so surprised when he comes.'

"'All right, Grandie,' Lucy said, 'I'll try to be patient. I do love surprises.'"

"With that, Lucy's grandfather walked away. She watched him talk cheerfully to everyone in the room. Soon, Lucy forgot about waiting for Santa. She joined the rest of the party and the fun. Lucy watched the men and women dancing. Then she ate some of the delicious food her mother had prepared for the guests.

"After the night's last song, Lucy's grandfather hugged her and wished her a Merry Christmas. Lucy kissed her grandfather on the cheek. Only then did she realize it was close to midnight.

"'Oh, Grandie,' Lucy said, 'the time flew by when I wasn't thinking about Santa. I had more fun, too. I can't believe it's midnight already.'

"Lucy's grandfather just smiled."

"Did the girl go to sleep without looking to see if Santa had come?" Sally asks.

"Not exactly," Grandma replies.

"As the last guests said goodnight, Lucy peeked at the Christmas tree, hoping new presents would be there. All she saw were the few gifts her family had put there. She was going to wait there next to the fireplace. But soon she heard her mother's voice. Lucy ran to the stairs.

"'Time for bed!' Lucy's mother called. 'If you don't go to sleep now, Santa may never come. He only comes when you are sleeping.'

"Lucy's father carried her up to bed. With each step, Lucy felt more tired. And before they reached her room, Lucy was fast asleep."

"Then, during the night, Lucy awoke. She rubbed her eyes and thought she heard sleigh bells jingling in the distance. Far off she heard a hearty 'Ho! Ho! Ho!' The voice sounded so familiar.

"'Grandie?' Lucy thought. But she was half asleep. 'No, it couldn't be.' Lucy soon fell back to sleep. In the morning, she would find new presents under the tree and a note from Santa."

As she finishes her story, Grandma looks down at Sally. She has drifted off to sleep. Wishing her happy dreams, Grandma pulls up Sally's covers and turns out the light. She walks downstairs to place a small wreath on the mantle for Santa. She thinks about herself all those years ago when she was the little girl in the story.

Grandma looks at the wreath over the fireplace.
Then she remembers her Grandie, the gentleman
with the shining eyes and unmistakable voice.
Could he really be Santa?

"It's possible," she says to herself.

CHRISTMAS GIFTS

Written by Suzanne Lieurance

Illustrated by Deborah Colvin Borgo

It was Christmas Eve in the snowy barnyard. Seven ordinary animals had just settled down for the night. It was just another ordinary night — or so they thought.

The hour of midnight drew near. Snow fell gently and silently to the ground. And then something quite amazing happened. These seven ordinary animals, in this simple barn, became seven special animals, if only for this one night.

"What has happened?" asked the young sheep. "Baa! Baa! I can talk!"

"Me, too!" said the dog. "Ruff! Ruff!"

"Moo-oo! Listen to me!" said the little calf.

"What's going on?" asked the surprised donkey. "Hee-haw!"

The cow was not surprised. "It's midnight," she said. "And it's Christmas Eve."

"What does that mean?" asked the sheep.

"I'll tell you a story," said the cow, "about the very first Christmas. Then you will understand."

All the animals in the barn gathered to hear the cow's story.

"Long, long ago, one special night," began the cow, "Baby Jesus was born in an ordinary stable, in an ordinary town called Bethlehem. This was the first Christmas."

"Was the stable like this barn?" the dog asked.

"Yes," said the cow, "almost exactly like it."

"With animals in the stable, just like us?" asked the young calf.

"Yes," said the cow, "with animals just like us. Let me explain.

"Before Baby Jesus was born, his mother, Mary, and her husband, Joseph, had to travel through the countryside to the town of Bethlehem. Their trip took many days. They traveled up and down steep hills. To make things easier for Mary, an ordinary donkey carried her on his back on this long trip, and Joseph led the way."

"A donkey, just like me?" asked the donkey.

"Yes, a donkey just like you," said the cow.

"Finally, Mary and Joseph arrived in Bethlehem. But there was nowhere for them to sleep. They had to go to a stable and sleep with the animals. The donkey carried Mary safely to that stable."

"So it was an ordinary donkey who gave Baby Jesus a precious and unique gift, even before he was born, by carrying Mary safely to Bethlehem.

"Later that evening, inside the simple stable, Mary gave birth to a special baby named Jesus.

"The stable was cold. Luckily, in the stable lived a handsome sheep with very soft, beautiful wool."

"A sheep, like me?" asked the little sheep.

"Yes, just like you and your mother," answered the cow. "And this sheep's soft, beautiful wool was made into a very special blanket. The sheep offered this blanket, her unique and most precious gift, to the baby. Mary wrapped Baby Jesus in this special, soft, woolly blanket. It would keep the baby snug and safe during his stay in the stable."

"After their long journey, and the birth of the baby, Mary and Joseph were too tired for lullabies. They needed something to lull the baby to sleep. But what? Mary and Joseph were lucky to find a gentle dove living high in the rafters of the stable."

"A dove, just like me?" asked the dove.

"Just like you," said the cow. "And each night her soft cooing soothed the animals in the barn so they could enjoy a good night's sleep. That night the white dove began to coo very softly. This cooing quickly lulled Baby Jesus to sleep, as he lay covered with the sheep's special, soft, woolly blanket.

"But the baby Jesus still didn't have everything he needed, even with these most precious and unique Christmas gifts."

"Since Baby Jesus was so special, someone was needed to keep watch over him and his family. A brave dog lived in the stable. And though he wasn't very big, he was a very special watchdog."

"Just like me!" said the dog.

"Yes, just like you," said the cow. "All night, this brave dog stood watch at the door to the stable. No harm would come to Baby Jesus as long as he was around. The dog was glad to offer this precious and unique gift and protect the baby from danger.

"All the animals in the stable gathered around Baby Jesus to adore him. Covered with a special blanket, lulled to sleep by the gentle cooing of the dove, the baby still needed some place very special to sleep."

"His mother could not hold him in her arms all night. So Mary needed a comfortable bed for her child. The ordinary cow came forward and offered the manger, her most precious and unique gift, so the baby would have a safe and soft place to rest his sweet head."

"An ordinary cow, just like you and me, Mom?" asked the young calf.

"Yes, just like you and me, dear," said the cow. "Mary and Joseph lined the manger with hay and tucked Baby Jesus under the soft woolen blanket.

"That night, something else happened that was special," continued the cow. "A bright star began to shine in the sky."

The animals were puzzled again.

"But where did that star come from?" asked the young calf.

"The star was a gift from God. It was there to announce to the world that a special baby had been born. It was the largest star in the sky. It shone over the earth to lead travelers from far and near to the Baby Jesus. In fact, the star was so bright, the stable glowed as the dog stood watch, with the cow and the donkey right nearby.

"So you see," said the cow, "it was on a special night, in a simple stable like this one, that ordinary animals became special animals. And they became special animals because of the unique and precious Christmas gifts each of them offered to Baby Jesus."

The animals gathered closer to the cow.

"It was a donkey, like me, who carried the baby's mother safely on his back," said the donkey.

"And a sheep, like me, gave the baby a special woolen blanket," said the young sheep.

"Only a dove, like me, could have lulled the baby to sleep," cooed the dove.

"And it took a brave dog to keep watch over them all," said the dog, "just like me. Ruff! Ruff!"

"Yes, everyone has a unique and most special gift to give at Christmas," said the cow. "That is why animals like us are given this special gift of speech each Christmas Eve at midnight. So we might tell our children about those very first Christmas gifts given by ordinary animals."

The animals gathered at the door to the stable.

Suddenly they saw a bright star in the sky.

"Look! It's the same star shining in the sky!" said the young donkey.

"Yes," said the cow. "A special star, to always remind us of that special night the most special baby was born."

THE NIGHT BEFORE CHRISTMAS

Written by Clement C. Moore

Illustrated by Tom Newsom

'Twas the night before Christmas,

when all through the house

Not a creature was stirring,

not even a mouse.

The stockings were hung

by the chimney with care,

In hopes that St. Nicholas

soon would be there.

The children were nestled

all snug in their beds,

While visions of sugarplums

danced in their heads.

And Mama in her kerchief,

and I in my cap,

Had just settled our brains

for a long winter's nap,

When out on the lawn

there arose such a clatter,

I sprang from my bed

to see what was the matter.

Away to the window

I flew like a flash,

Tore open the shutters

and threw up the sash.

The moon on the breast

of the new-fallen snow

Gave a luster of midday

to objects below.

When what to my wondering eyes

should appear

But a miniature sleigh

and eight tiny reindeer.

With a little old driver,

so lively and quick,

I knew in a moment

it must be St. Nick!

More rapid than eagles

his coursers they came,

And he whistled and shouted

and called them by name:

"Now, Dasher! Now, Dancer!

Now, Prancer and Vixen!

On, Comet! On, Cupid!

On, Donder and Blitzen!

To the top of the porch!

To the top of the wall!

Now dash away! Dash away!

Dash away, all!"

As dry leaves that before

the wild hurricane fly,

When they meet with an obstacle,

mount to the sky,

So up to the housetop

the coursers they flew,

With a sleigh full of toys—

and St. Nicholas, too.

And then, in a twinkling,

I heard on the roof

The prancing and pawing

of each little hoof.

As I drew in my head

and was turning around,

Down the chimney St. Nicholas

came with a bound.

He was dressed all in fur,

from his head to his foot,

And his clothes were all tarnished

with ashes and soot.

Abundle of toys

he had flung on his back,

And he looked like a peddler

just opening his pack.

His eyes, how they twinkled!

His dimples, how merry!

His cheeks were like roses,

his nose like a cherry!

His droll little mouth

was drawn up like a bow,

And the beard on his chin was

as white as the snow.

The stump of a pipe

he held tight in his teeth,

And the smoke,

it encircled his head like a wreath.

He had a broad face

and a little round belly

That shook, when he laughed,

like a bowl full of jelly.

He was chubby and plump,

a right jolly old elf,

And I laughed when I saw him,

in spite of myself.

A wink of his eye

and a twist of his head

Soon gave me to know

I had nothing to dread.

He spoke not a word,

but went straight to his work,

And filled all the stockings,

then turned with a jerk,

And laying a finger

aside of his nose,

And giving a nod,

up the chimney he rose.

He sprang to his sleigh,

to his team gave a whistle,

And away they all flew

like the down of a thistle.

But I heard him exclaim,

ere he drove out of sight,

"Happy Christmas to all,

and to all a good night!"

THE TAILOR'S APPRENTICES

Written by Leslie Lindecker

Illustrated by Mike Jaroszko

Back in the days when men wore beautiful clothes and wigs, there was a poor tailor. He worked diligently and spent all of his money on lovely fabrics. He worked from dawn to the last light of dusk, making beautiful garments for the citizens of the town. Although his own coat was quite threadbare and popping at the seams, the coats he made for the townsfolk featured fine silk and satin, warm velvet and corduroy.

As he snipped and stitched, the tailor talked to the mice who lived beneath the floor. A little mouse hopped onto the end of the tailor's worktable. The tailor smiled and said, "Someday my hard work will be rewarded. Until then, you must appreciate the bits and ends that are too small for me to use."

The mouse winked at the tailor. Then he daintily picked up a bit of ribbon from the table, scrambled to the floor, and disappeared into the woodwork. The tailor laughed softly to himself and continued to sew. "I wonder what he'll make," thought the tailor.

On the very day the good mayor of the town announced his wedding was to be on Christmas Day, the tailor received a request from the mayor for a special new suit.

The tailor danced with glee. The mice peeked out from under his table to see what was happening.

"My little friends," the tailor said, "you shall have the finest bits of lace and thread, because I am going to make the mayor's suit for his wedding on Christmas Day! It shall be of my best emerald satin, embroidered and stitched with gold. I shall make a beautiful vest also, all trimmed with lace. A happy day, indeed!"

The mice squealed in agreement and scurried out from under the tailor's dancing feet. The tailor measured and marked, and measured again. He cut out the coat from the emerald cloth and trimmed it carefully with small snips. He spun the cloth around and measured once again.

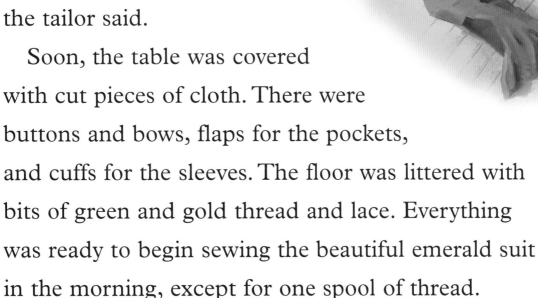

"No waste on this fabric. Just enough for a suit for a mouse, and such a grand suit that would be, all stitched with gold!" the tailor said.

Soon, the table was covered with cut pieces of cloth. There were buttons and bows, flaps for the pockets, and cuffs for the sleeves. The floor was littered with bits of green and gold thread and lace. Everything was ready to begin sewing the beautiful emerald suit in the morning, except for one spool of thread.

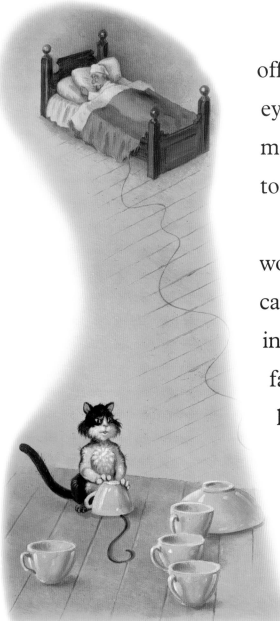

The tailor heaved a sigh, took off his spectacles, and rubbed his eyes. "We will begin again in the morning, my friends. It is too dark to sew tonight."

The tailor pulled on his old, worn-out coat, snuffed out the lit candle, and stepped out of his shop into the snowy December night. He fastened the window latch and locked the door, putting the key into his pocket. He shuffled through the snow and up the rickety stairs to the room he rented above his shop.

The tailor lived alone with his cat, whom he called Tomkin. As he unlocked the door, Tomkin meowed.

"Tomkin, old friend," said the tailor, "fortune has finally smiled upon us, but I am worn out beyond working this night."

The tailor built up the fire in the grate, then took a scrap of paper and made a list. "Tomkin, I need you to go to the shopkeeper. We need a bottle of milk, a bit of bread, and I must have a spool of golden thread for the mayor's new suit. Please don't forget the golden thread." The tailor tied the list and his last dollar to Tomkin's collar, then opened the door for the cat.

Tomkin walked slowly into the dark, cold night. Although he was usually a faithful cat, Tomkin wasn't fond of the cold. In fact, he hated the cold.

Instead of milk, bread, and a spool of golden thread, Tomkin had mice on his mind. Tomkin spent much of his time chasing the fast, crafty mice. They were often too fast for him. He would run and pounce at them, but they would slip away under the floorboards.

That day, Tomkin was especially fortunate. He had caught many mice that morning. Saving them for his supper, Tomkin trapped the small mice under bowls and cups. At least after his long walk in the cold, he would enjoy a fine meal.

The tailor was very tired. "I fear I've a touch of the flu," he said as he felt his forehead. He went to bed and thought about the mayor's new suit. Feverish, the tailor reached out to touch the emerald fabric and the crisp, white lace. He imagined the most beautiful suit.

"The mayor will be pleased when he wears this fine suit," he said to himself. "The finest suit, fit for a mayor on Christmas Day."

Suddenly the tailor heard a tip-tip-tap coming from somewhere in the small room. It was the faintest of tip-tip-taps, but the tailor went to investigate. He searched under the bed. He searched under the sink. He searched under the table. He could see nothing, but he continued to hear the tip-tip-tapping. The sound was the loudest at the side of the sink.

At the sink, his teacups and mugs, bowls and pots were all turned upside down. From under one of the teacups he heard the tip-tip-tap again.

Slowly the tailor lifted the teacup, and out popped a lovely lady mouse. She smiled and soon scampered away. The tailor took off his spectacles and rubbed his eyes. Then he heard a scritch-scritch-scratch. He looked under a bowl and was met with the gaze of a handsome gentleman mouse, who bowed to the tailor before running away.

"I truly must be ill, for I swear that mouse was wearing a hat!" exclaimed the tailor. "I do believe my dear old Tomkin has been very busy, and I don't think he captured these mice for company!" The tailor began to turn over all the teacups and mugs.

He found many little mice hopping and bobbing and running about.

The tailor continued to talk to himself while he prepared for bed. "Ah, the mayor's suit shall be my finest creation," he said. "But will I be able to finish it by Christmas Day?"

The little mice listened to the tailor as he muttered on about the suit for the mayor. Suddenly, they began to squeak and scamper. Then they all ran away and hid under the floorboards.

Tomkin nudged open the door and walked in with a gust of cold air. He hated snow, and it was in his ears. He jumped up on the table and dropped the sack he had been carrying in his mouth. It contained the bottle of milk and the bit of bread.

Then Tomkin spied the overturned teacups. With an angry cat snarl, he jumped onto the sink. The last little mice scurried to the floor and ran away.

"Tomkin, old friend," the tailor said from his bed. "Did you get my spool of golden thread?"

Being in an ill-tempered mood, Tomkin hid the spool of thread under the teapot lid. He jumped up onto the tailor's bed and kneaded the quilt with his claws. Then Tomkin hunted throughout the room for even one of the mice he had captured. Tomkin looked behind doors and under the bed, but not one mouse was to be found. The two of them made a strange chorus that night with the tailor feverishly muttering about his golden thread, accompanied by Tomkin meowing and growling for his little lost mice.

The tailor was feeling very sick and stayed in bed for several days, tossing and turning with fever. He mumbled about the mayor's suit and the spool of thread.

Christmas Day was fast approaching, and he was too ill to work. Tomkin mewed for the little mice, and he fed on the bit of bread and milk he had fetched a few days before. How he wanted those mice!

Christmas Eve came and the townsfolk scurried about in preparation for Christmas Day. No one thought of the tailor's shop and the mayor's fine suit.

Later that night, the animals in the town lifted their voices to celebrate. However, Tomkin only heard the voices coming from inside the tailor's shop.

Tomkin went down the rickety steps and into the snow to see what was happening. From the window ledge he peeked into the shop. In the candlelight, Tomkin could see his little brown mice, singing and dancing, and sewing!

They were stitching the beautiful emerald coat with the golden thread and wonderful lace.

Tomkin yowled through the window at the mice. They jumped, then giggled and waved at the cat who was peeking through the glass. They continued to sew and dance to their songs, keeping time with the click of their thimbles. Tomkin tried to pull the latch on the door, but the key was resting safely in the pocket of the tailor's old coat and Tomkin couldn't get in.

Fascinated, Tomkin watched the little mice sew the mayor's new suit. Near dawn, he heard the mice cry in chorus, "No more golden thread!" Then the mice ran away.

Tomkin jumped down from the window ledge and climbed the steps to the tailor's tiny room. He dropped the spool of thread on the tailor's bed.

"Tomkin! You did get my thread," said the tailor. He jumped up from bed. "It's Christmas Day, and what will the mayor do for his suit?" he cried.

The tailor hurried down the steps to the shop. As he opened the door, the tailor shouted for joy. For there on the table was the loveliest suit. Everything was finished except for one tiny buttonhole. There was a scrap of paper pinned to the buttonhole that read "No more golden thread." The tailor danced about, then finished the buttonhole.

Thus began the long and good fortune of Tomkin and the tailor, who grew quite rich.

JINGLE BELLS

Written by Sarah Toast

Illustrated by Kathleen O'Malley

Andrew and his sister Arabella live in town. Andrew works in Mr. Ward's store, and Arabella teaches school. Their family—Mother, Father, Ned, Sue, and Grandpa—all live on the farm where Andrew and Arabella grew up.

It is Christmas Eve. Andrew and Arabella have been planning a wonderful Christmas surprise for their family. Andrew asks Mr. Ward if he can borrow his horse, Nelly, and the sleigh.

"Why, certainly!" says Mr. Ward. "It will be my Christmas gift to you."

Andrew walks to Mr. Ward's stable. He puts a leather strap with jingle bells on Nelly's tail and ties a bright red ribbon around her neck. Then he leads her out into the snow.

Andrew hitches up the sleigh. He tosses in a warm blanket and guides Nelly out of the gate. He and Nelly pass a watchful snowman as they glide toward town to get Arabella. The sun is just starting to set in the early evening sky.

The bells on Nelly's tail jingle and jangle with the rhythm of her prancing steps. Andrew whistles "Jingle Bells" as the sleigh glides along the snowy path. He admires the Christmas wreaths hanging on each front door.

Arabella has had to work today, too. But now she waits anxiously for Andrew at the boarding house where she lives. Her spirits are bright with happiness at the thought of their Christmas surprise. She peeks out the window to look for Andrew.

The lights are coming on in the houses in town as Nelly pulls Andrew down the center of Main Street. The horse has to pull harder through the drifting piles of snow.

Andrew thinks about how far it is to the farm, where his family is gathered together for Christmas. Even aunts, uncles, and cousins are visiting at the farm for the holiday.

At the end of the street, Andrew passes a small group of Christmas carolers. They make their way from house to house singing songs of Christmas joy. Nelly's jingling bells add some cheerful music to the carolers' songs. Andrew smiles as he passes the singers. He slows down as he comes to the boarding house where Arabella stays.

Andrew stops outside the boarding house. He hitches Nelly to the post.

Arabella quickly puts on her hat and gloves. Then she runs to the door before Andrew can even ring the bell.

"Andrew, do you think they know we're coming?" Arabella asks.

"No," he says. "They know that we worked today. They wouldn't expect us tonight."

Nelly swishes her tail, jingling the bells, as Andrew takes Arabella's hand. He helps Arabella climb up into the sleigh.

"I'm so glad we sent our presents already," says Arabella with a twinkle. "That will surely make them think we couldn't come."

Snow continues to fall softly as Andrew and Arabella head for the farm.

"I'm so eager to see Mother and Father and Grandpa again," says Andrew.

"And little Ned and Sue, too," says Arabella. "Do you think they will like all of the nice presents we sent to them?"

"We will get to see when they open the presents, won't we?" Andrew replies. "With any luck, we'll be home before they even wake up! Won't they be so surprised?"

The sky is getting darker as night falls, but the starlight and moonlight twinkling on the snow make the night bright and sparkly. Nelly doesn't need a lantern to find her way.

Andrew and Arabella talk of Christmases when they were little as Nelly pulls them home. They remember their favorite Christmas gifts. Then they sing their favorite Christmas songs and laugh when the jingling bells don't match their song.

Around midnight, clouds blow across the bright face of the moon. The stars are hidden, as well. Andrew and Arabella are not even halfway home yet, and they are nearing the deep woods.

Among the trees, it is difficult to see the road. The deep woods is a very dark place. But Nelly is strong and seems to know the way.

"I knew I'd seen Nelly before," says Arabella. "She's from the horse farm next to Mother and Father's farm!"

It isn't long before all the clouds disappear. The moonlight reflects brightly off the snow. But the late hour and the rhythm of the jingling bells are making Arabella and Andrew sleepy.

"Andrew, how about if I take a turn at the reins so you can take a nap?" suggests Arabella.

"Are you sure?" asks Andrew. "It might be a little slippery out here."

"Yes," says Arabella. "I have been looking forward to driving Nelly."

Soon only the sound of Nelly's bells breaks the deep silence. Arabella marvels at the purple shadows cast on the snow in the moonlight. She is filled with awe by the haloed stars that crowd the beautiful Christmas Eve sky.

Later, an owl hoots and Andrew awakens. He is refreshed from his long nap.

"Your turn to sleep, Arabella," says Andrew. He takes the reins from her, and Arabella naps. Nelly seems to speed up as they come closer to home.

Arabella awakens as the sky brightens to greet Christmas Day.

"We're almost there, Andrew!" she exclaims when she sees the familiar shape of the family farmhouse ahead. "I can't wait to surprise our family on Christmas morning!"

It isn't long before they turn onto the road that leads up to their gate. Already there is a light on in the kitchen. Mother is always up first. She is making hot chocolate and coffee.

Sleepy faces peer out of the windows as Nelly brings the sleigh right up to the door. Mother runs out to hug Arabella and Andrew.

"My goodness! We didn't think you would be home for Christmas this year!" says Mother.

The windows fly open, and voices young and old shout, "Merry Christmas, Andrew! Merry Christmas, Arabella!"

What a merry Christmas surprise!

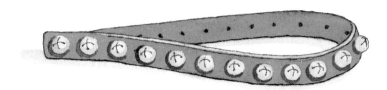

THE
NUTCRACKER

Written by E. T. A. Hoffman

Illustrated by Linda Dockey Graves

On Christmas Eve, Dr. Stahlbaum's children were not allowed to set foot in the parlor. Fritz and Clara sat together in the back room and waited. "Oh, what do you think Godfather Drosselmeier has made for us?" asked Clara.

Fritz said it was a fortress with lots of soldiers.

"No," Clara interrupted. "It's a beautiful garden with a big lake and lovely swans swimming around."

"Godfather Drosselmeier can't make a garden," said Fritz rather rudely.

At that moment, a bell rang, the doors flew open, and a flood of light streamed in from the big parlor. "Come in, dear children," said Papa and Mama.

The children stood in awe. Then Clara cried out, "Oh, how lovely! The tree is spectacular!"

Meanwhile, Fritz galloped around the table, trying out the new horse he had found. Then he reviewed his new squadron of soldiers.

Just then, the bell rang again. Knowing that Godfather Drosselmeier would be unveiling his present, the children ran to a table near the wall. There, they found a magnificent castle with lots of sparkling windows and towers.

Fritz looked at the toy children dancing in the castle, then said, "Godfather Drosselmeier, I want to go inside your castle."

"Impossible," said Godfather Drosselmeier.

"Then make the children come out," cried Fritz.

"No," said their godfather crossly, "that, too, is impossible. This is how the mechanism works."

"Then I don't like it," said Fritz. "My soldiers march as I command, and they're not stuck in a house." Fritz marched away to play with his soldiers.

Clara did not leave the Christmas table. She had just caught sight of something.

When Fritz marched away, an excellent little man came into view. The distinction of his dress showed him to be a man of taste and breeding. Oddly enough, he wore a skimpy cloak that was made of wood. His green eyes were full of kindness, and his cotton beard was most becoming.

"Oh, Father!" Clara cried out. "Who does that little man belong to?"

"Dear child," said Dr. Stahlbaum, "our friend here will serve you well. He will crack nuts for you."

Dr. Stahlbaum carefully lifted his wooden cloak, and the little man opened his mouth wide, revealing two rows of sharp white teeth. Clara put in a nut, and—crack—the little man bit it in two. The shell fell down, and Clara found the kernel in her hand.

Fritz ran over to his sister. He chose the biggest nut, and all of a sudden—crack, crack—three little teeth fell out of the Nutcracker's mouth.

"Oh, my poor little Nutcracker!" Clara cried.

"He calls himself a nutcracker," said Fritz, "but his teeth are no good. Give him to me, Clara."

Clara was in tears. "No!" she cried. "He's mine, and you can't have him." Clara wrapped the Nutcracker in her handkerchief and bandaged his wounded mouth. Then she rocked him in her arms like a baby.

It was getting late. Mother urged her children to go to bed. But Clara pleaded, "Just a little while longer, Mother."

Clara's mother put out all of the candles, leaving on only one lamp. "Go to bed soon," she said, "or you won't be able to get up tomorrow."

"Thank you," Clara said smiling.

As soon as Clara was alone, she set the poor Nutcracker carefully on the table.

Clara unwrapped the handkerchief ever so slowly and examined his wounds.

"Nutcracker," she said softly, "I'm going to take care of you until you're well and happy again."

Clara picked up the Nutcracker and placed him next to the other toys in the parlor cabinet. She was going to her bedroom when she heard whispering and shuffling. The clock whirred twelve times. Then she heard a thousand tiny feet scampering behind the walls. Soon Clara saw mice all over the room. Noisily they formed ranks, just like Fritz's soldiers.

Crushed stone flew out of the floor as though driven by some underground force, and seven mouse heads with seven sparkling crowns rose up, squeaking and squealing hideously.

This enormous mouse, with seven heads, was hailed by the entire army. And then the army set itself in motion—hop, hop, trot, trot—heading straight for the toy cabinet.

At the same time, Clara saw a strange glow inside the toy cabinet. All at once, the Nutcracker jumped from the cabinet, and the squeaking and squealing started again.

"Trusty Vassal-Drummer," cried the Nutcracker, "sound the advance!" He played so loudly that the windows of the toy cabinet rattled. A clattering was heard from inside, and all the boxes containing Fritz's army burst open. Soldiers climbed out and jumped to the bottom shelf. Then they formed ranks on the floor.

The Nutcracker ran up and down, shouting words of encouragement to the troops.

A few moments later, guns roared boom! boom! There was so much smoke and dust that Clara could hardly see what was happening. Then the mice brought up more troops.

The Nutcracker found himself trapped against the toy cabinet. "Bring up the reserves!" he cried. A few men came out, but they wielded their swords so very clumsily.

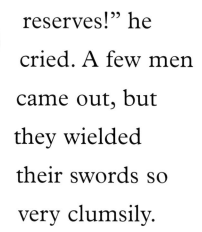

One of them knocked off the Nutcracker's cap! The Nutcracker was in dire peril. He tried to jump over the ledge of the cabinet, but his legs were too short. In despair he shouted, "A horse, a horse! My kingdom for a horse!"

At that moment, the Mouse King charged the Nutcracker. Without quite knowing what she was doing, Clara took off her left shoe and flung it with all her might. Then, everything vanished from Clara's sight. She fell to the floor.

When Clara awoke from her deep sleep, she was lying in her own little bed. The sun shining into the room sparkled on the ice-coated windowpanes. A strange gentleman was sitting beside her, but she soon recognized him as Dr. Wendelstern. "She's awake," he said softly to Clara's mother. She came over and gave Clara an anxious look.

"Oh, Mother dear," Clara whispered. "Have all the nasty mice gone away? Did I save the poor Nutcracker?"

Clara's mother sighed. "What have mice got to do with the Nutcracker? Oh, we've been very worried about you. Last night, I found you lying beside the toy cabinet in a faint. Your arm was bleeding terribly."

"Oh, Mother," Clara broke in. "There had just been a big battle between the toy soldiers and the mice. The mice were going to capture the poor Nutcracker. I threw my shoe at the mice, and after that I don't know what happened."

Clara's parents talked with Dr. Wendelstern. Clara had to stay in bed and take medicine for a week.

When Godfather Drosselmeier came to visit, he brought books and lovely sweets of every color. "I've brought you something else that will give you pleasure," he told Clara. With that, he reached into his pocket and took out the Nutcracker, whose lost teeth had been put back in very neatly and firmly, and whose broken jaw had been fixed as good as new. Clara cried out for joy!

That night, Clara was awakened by the sound of a thousand tiny feet. "Oh no, the mice!" Clara cried.

Then she saw the Mouse King squeeze through a hole in the wall. He scurried across the floor and jumped onto the table beside Clara's bed. "Give me your candy," he said, "or I'll bite your Nutcracker to pieces." Then he slipped back into the hole.

Clara was so frightened that she couldn't speak. She jumped out of her bed.

Then she put her whole supply of candy at the foot of her bed. By morning, every piece was gone. Clara was happy. She had saved her friend.

That night, however, the Mouse King returned. "Give me your most beautiful dress and all of your picture books," he hissed.

Clara was beside herself with anguish. The next morning she went to the Nutcracker and said, "What can I do? If I give the Mouse King all my books and my dress, he'll just keep asking for more."

The Nutcracker said in a strained whisper, "Find me a sword." At that, his words ebbed away and his eyes became fixed.

Clara asked Fritz for a sword, and Fritz slung it around the Nutcracker's waist.

The next night fear and dread kept Clara awake. At the stroke of twelve she heard clanging and crashing. Then suddenly, "Squeak!"

Soon Clara heard a soft knocking at the door and a faint little voice say, "Miss Stahlbaum, open the door and have no fear. I bring good news!"

Clara swiftly opened the door and found that the Nutcracker had turned into a prince!

The prince took Clara's hand and told her how he was really Godfather Drosselmeier's nephew, and an evil spell had turned him into a nutcracker. When he defeated the Mouse King, the spell was broken.

"Oh, Miss Stahlbaum," said the prince, "what great things I can show you in this hour of victory over my enemy, if you will follow me a little way."

Clara agreed and followed the prince to the big clothes cupboard in the entrance hall.

The prince stepped inside and climbed a little ladder into the sleeve of a coat. Clara climbed the ladder, too.

When Clara looked out through the neck hole of the coat, she found herself in a fragrant meadow.

"This is Candy Meadow," said the prince.

Looking up, Clara saw a magnificent arch. "It's so wonderful here," she sighed.

The prince clapped his hands, and a little shepherd appeared.

He brought up a golden chair and asked Clara to sit down. Then the young shepherd danced a ballet. Suddenly, as if at a signal, he vanished into the woods.

The prince took Clara's hand and led her on a tour of his kingdom. They walked through a grove, where icing lined the rooftops of each house. They walked across bridges and had a picnic in the Frosted Forest.

In the distance Clara saw a city with a giant castle.

"I have never seen anything so fantastic!" Clara exclaimed. "Can we go there?"

Suddenly, a gondola appeared. Clara and the prince were gently whisked away toward the city.

Clara saw a castle with a hundred lofty towers. "This," said the prince, "is Marzipan Castle." At that moment they heard soft music. The gates of the castle opened, and out stepped four ladies so richly attired that Clara knew they must be princesses. One by one, they embraced their brother. The ladies led Clara and the prince into the castle. Then they prepared a meal for Clara and the prince. They brought in the most wonderful fruit and candy Clara had ever seen. Then they began to squeeze the fruit and grate sugared almonds.

The most beautiful of the prince's sisters handed her a little golden mortar and said, "Dear sweet friend, would you care to pound some rock candy?"

While Clara pounded away, the prince told the history of the cruel war between the Mouse King's army and his own.

As Clara listened to his story, she began to feel very dizzy. The room began to spin, and Clara felt as though she were-falling. Clara fell to the floor.

When she opened her eyes, Clara was lying in her little bed. Her mother was standing over her.

"Clara,
how in the
world can anyone
sleep so long!" her
mother exclaimed.
"Oh, Mother," said
Clara, "you cannot imagine all
of the wonderful places that young
Mr. Drosselmeier took me to last night."
Clara's mother looked at her in disbelief.
"You've had a long, beautiful dream,"
she said. "That is all."
"But Mother," said Clara, "the Nutcracker is really
young Mr. Drosselmeier, Godfather Drosselmeier's
nephew. And he is a prince, too!"

Mrs. Stahlbaum burst out laughing. "You're to forget all about this foolishness." So Clara did.

One day Clara's mother said, "Your godfather's nephew is here. So be on your best behavior."

Clara turned as red as a beet when she saw the young man. Then he asked her to go with him to the cabinet in the parlor. He went down on one knee and said, "Miss Stahlbaum, you see at your feet the happiest of young men, whose life you saved on this very spot. Please promise me that one day you will come and reign with me over Marzipan Castle."

Clara said, "Of course I will come with you."

Years later, Clara left in a carriage. She is still the queen of a country where the most wonderful things can be seen if you have the right sort of eyes for it.

CHRISTMAS SOCKS

Written by Sarah Toast

Illustrated by Debbie Pinkney

It is Christmas Eve. Santa and his elves have been working hard all year to make toys and dolls for children all over the world.

Santa's big bag is packed so full. It is overflowing with drums and bears, dolls and balls—all sorts of things to delight children on Christmas morning.

"But Santa," says an elf. "How does your bag hold a toy for every child?"

"Ho, ho, ho!" says Santa with a laugh. "When I leave gifts under the Christmas trees, magic fills my bag up again!"

"That's amazing, Santa!" says the elf.

Just then, Mrs. Claus dashes out of the house. "My dear, don't forget the candy for all the Christmas stockings!"

"Thank you very much!" says Santa. He climbs into his sleigh. His sleigh is so full that Mrs. Claus can barely see Santa!

In one house below, David and Molly are fast asleep. They are dreaming a wonderful dream of Santa and his reindeer flying through the sky to their house.

David and Molly had written a letter to Santa with their secret Christmas wish in it. It took them a long time to write the letter. They wanted to make sure they didn't forget anything. When David and Molly had finished their letter, they showed it to their mother.

"Now that your letter is done, I'll help you bake Christmas cookies. Then you can leave your letter for Santa next to the cookies so he will be sure to see," said Mom.

After the gooey cookies came out of the oven, Molly and David decorated them. Before the two children went to bed that night, they piled cookies on a big plate. Next to it they put a glass of cold milk and their letter.

"Santa won't be able to miss it," said David.

Now the two children are sound asleep in their beds as Santa's journey brings him closer to their house with each stop he makes.

At last Santa arrives at the rooftop of David and Molly's house. The reindeer land so softly on the roof that there's not even a bump, just the faint sound of jingle bells.

Snug in their beds in the bedroom below, David and Molly dream all night about their very special request.

"The chimney looks a little snug," Santa says. Santa has to fit down the narrow chimney with his big bag of toys and a special something tucked in his jacket.

"I'm not sure I can make it," says Santa as he measures the opening. But with a deep breath and a little Christmas magic, he slides down the chimney with hardly a scrape. He manages to fit his big belly, big pack of toys, and all.

Santa looks around. "What a nice tree. I bet David and Molly helped to decorate it."

Santa looks through his bag for the presents for David and Molly. At the bottom of the bag, he finally finds their presents. Santa puts the presents underneath the tree for David and Molly. Then he thinks to himself, "Goodness, I've gone many miles already tonight, and I'm getting a bit hungry! Can't stop yet, though. I've got more to do here before I can have a bit of a rest."

Santa arranges the presents, then looks through his great big bag one more time.

Then Santa goes over to the mantle where the stockings are hung. "Now, where are Mrs. Claus's candies?" he thinks. Santa reaches inside his pack for the candies.

Santa fills all the stockings with candy canes, peppermint sticks, cinnamon balls, and other yummy Christmas goodies. Even Mom and Dad get Mrs. Claus's candy treats.

At last, Santa pats the special something tucked in his jacket and says, "Now for a treat!"

Santa looks around and sees the plate of cookies and glass of milk sitting on the small table.

"Ah!" says Santa. "I knew it! Molly and David are such good children. They have left out a big plate of Christmas cookies for me. That's just what I need to finish my deliveries to all the other good, little children on my list."

But before Santa takes a bite, he goes to the kitchen and brings back a saucer. Then he pours some of the milk into the saucer and sets it on the floor. He unbuttons his jacket and says, "Come on out and have some milk!"

Santa leans back in a chair and enjoys the yummy cookies. He eats almost all the cookies on the plate and drinks the rest of his milk.

Then Santa picks up the letter from Molly and David.

Santa's eyes twinkle. "I already know what this says," he chuckles. "I knew it as soon as they wrote the letter!"

"To Santa," the letter begins. "We have been good all year. We have helped our Mom and Dad a lot. We took care of Mrs. Jasper's cat when she was away. We really liked the cat. So, we read books about how to take care of a pet."

"Will you please bring us a cat for Christmas," continues the letter. "We will take good care of it and love it." The letter is signed, "From your friends, Molly and David."

Santa picks up the empty saucer and takes it to the kitchen. When he returns, he says, "Did you enjoy your milk, Socks?"

Socks answers with a contented purr. Then she settles down to dream sweet cat dreams about a nice boy and girl who will play with her.

Santa gives a merry wave with his mittens as he bounds up the chimney.

David and Molly wake up Christmas morning and hurry downstairs.

"Hooray! Santa brought us a cat, just like we wanted!" David and Molly look at each other and say, "Let's name our new kitty Socks."

THE PERFECT TREE

Written by Suzanne Lieurance

Illustrated by Kathleen O'Malley

A little pine tree grows in the forest. "The big pine trees are the prettiest trees," the little pine says to himself.

It is Christmastime in the forest, and all the trees are excited about the season. Their thick branches are covered with blankets of snow—all the branches except for the little pine's, that is.

"Who would want such a little tree with such thin branches?" he says.

"Now don't you worry," says the biggest spruce in the forest, "someone will think you're special."

"All of you trees are special," chirps a little bird, sitting on a snowy bough.

But the little pine isn't so sure. His branches start to droop a little.

"Hey, wait for me!" Sarah calls. "I want to pick the tree this year!"

Her brother David scoops up some soft snow and makes a perfectly round snowball.

"Not if I get there first," he shouts. He throws the snowball at a lamppost, then runs as fast as he can through the snow.

Dad and Mom follow as they all start out on a snowy walk to the forest.

"Remember," says Mom, "it can't be too broad, or it won't fit through the door."

"And it can't be too tall," says David, "or it will scrape the ceiling."

"We'll know the perfect tree when we see it," says Sarah.

Soon the family arrives in the middle of the forest. The trees are feeling very nervous. They can't wait to see which tree will be picked.

The children race right past all the giant spruce trees. They stop at the little pine.

"This one!" decides Sarah.

"Yeah! It's perfect!" says David.

The children dance around the little pine.

"Hmm," says Mom, "not too broad."

"And it won't scrape the ceiling," says Sarah.

"Looks just right to me," says Dad.

"See," says the biggest spruce, "someone thinks you're special already."

"They can't mean me," says the little pine. "Look at my thin little branches."

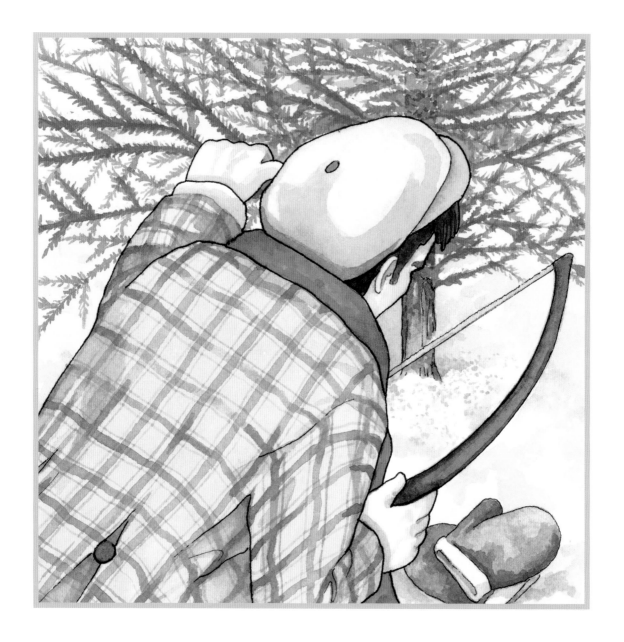

Dad examines the tree closely. "The trunk is not very broad. It'll be easy to cut," he says.

"Be careful," says Mom.

"I'll be very careful," says Dad. "I won't hurt our special tree a bit."

Dad begins to saw at the bottom of the little pine's trunk.

"What beautiful, straight branches," says Mom. "Such a lovely little tree."

"See? They don't think your branches are too skinny," says the largest spruce. "They think you're special and beautiful."

The little pine's branches still droop. Then the little pine says, "They think I'm special now. But wait till they get me home."

Once the little pine is cut, Dad carefully wraps it with twine.

"The twine makes sure the branches won't bend and break off," he tells the children. Sarah and Dad lead the way home with their new tree tied securely onto the sled.

"Where will we put the tree?" asks David.

"In front of the window," says Mom, "so everyone can see our perfect little tree."

"The decorations will be so beautiful," Sarah says, "our tree will be the best one ever!" She runs ahead to get out the decorations.

"I hope the decorations look right on my skinny little brances," the little pine thinks. "I don't want to disappoint my new family."

At home, Dad and David make a tree stand for the little pine. Dad puts a bowl of water near the bottom of the tree's trunk.

"What's that for?" asks David.

"To give the tree a drink," says Dad. "We need to take care of our perfect little tree."

Sarah and Mom watch as Dad and David get everything ready.

"Look," says Sarah. "People can see our tree from both front windows."

"You're right," says Mom. "Everyone will get to admire our special tree."

"Oh no," thought the little pine. "Everyone will see how silly the decorations look on me! I hope they don't stand outside the window and laugh."

Mom gets up from her chair. "It's time to start decorating," she says.

"What can we do?" Sarah and David ask.

"You can start with these," says Mom, scooting some boxes near the tree. Inside the boxes are bright ornaments of all shapes, sizes, and colors.

"Ooh, they are so shiny," says Sarah.

"We must be very careful. Some of these were Grandma's favorite ornaments," says Mom. "We don't want to break any of them."

"What a lucky tree," says David, "to wear such special ornaments."

"I'll place the angel on the top," says Dad.

The little pine is worried the angel will not be able to balance on his thin top branches.

David and Sarah hang shiny ornaments on the little pine's branches until the boxes are empty. Mom wraps the tree with garlands of red ribbon. The angel Dad placed atop the highest branch proudly watches over everything. The little pine's branches are still strong enough.

"Isn't it the most beautiful tree you have ever seen?" asks Sarah.

"It certainly is," says Dad.

"How lucky we were to find such a special tree," says David.

The little pine perks up. "Wait! The family isn't disappointed after all. Maybe the big spruce trees were right."

The family admires their beautiful tree.

David glances out the window. "Look!" he says. "It's snowing."

"This is the perfect Christmas," says Mom.

The little pine stands so very proud and straight. "The spruce trees were right," he thinks to himself. "Being special doesn't mean being the biggest or the most beautiful. In the forest, I thought that I was a scrawny little pine. But now I know that I truly am a special tree."

THE GIFT
OF THE MAGI

Written by O. Henry

Illustrated by Wendy Edelson

One dollar and eighty-seven cents. That was all. And sixty-seven cents of it was in pennies. Pennies saved one, two, and three at a time. Three times Della counted it. One dollar and eighty-seven cents. And the next day would be Christmas.

There was clearly nothing to do but flop down on the shabby little couch and howl. So Della did it. She was beginning to believe that life was made up mostly of sniffles. While the mistress of the home is gradually subsiding from the first stage to the second, take a look at the home. It was a furnished flat at $8 per week.

In the vestibule below there was a letterbox into which no letter would go. And there was an electric doorbell from which no mortal finger could coax a ring. Also there was a small card bearing the name "Mr. James Dillingham Young."

The "Dillingham" had been flung to the breeze during a former period of prosperity when its possessor was being paid $30 per week. Now, when the income was shrunk to $20, though, they were thinking seriously of contracting to a modest and unassuming "D." But whenever Mr. James Dillingham Young came home and reached his flat above he was called "Jim" and greatly hugged by Mrs. James Dillingham Young, already introduced to you as Della. Which is all very good.

Della stood by the window and looked out dully at a gray cat walking near a fence in the backyard. Tomorrow would be Christmas Day, and she had only $1.87 with which to buy Jim a present. She had been saving every penny she could for months, with this result. Twenty dollars a week does not go far.

Only $1.87 to buy a present for Jim. Many a happy hour she had spent planning for something nice for him, something fine and rare and sterling, something just a little bit near to being worthy of the honor of being owned by Jim.

There was a pier glass between the windows of the room. A very thin and very agile person may, by observing his reflection in the mirrored strips, obtain a fairly accurate conception of his looks.

Della,
being thin,
had mastered the
art. Suddenly she
whirled from the window
and stood before the glass. Her
eyes were shining, but her face had
lost its color. Rapidly she pulled down
her hair and let it fall to its full length.

Now, there were two possessions of the
James Dillingham Youngs in which
they both took a mighty pride.

One was Jim's gold watch that had been his
father's and grandfather's. The other was Della's
hair. So now Della's hair fell about her, shining like
a cascade of brown waters. It reached below her
waist and made itself almost a garment for her.

Then she did it up again nervously and quickly. On went her old brown jacket; on went her old brown hat. With a whirl of skirts and with the sparkle still in her eyes, she fluttered out the door and down the stairs.

Where she stopped the sign read: "Madame Sofronie. Hair Goods of All Kinds." One flight up Della ran. Madame Sofronie was large and chilly. She hardly looked the "Sofronie."

"Will you buy my hair?" asked Della.

"I buy hair," said Madame Sofronie. "Take yer hat off and let's have a sight at the looks of it."

Down rippled the brown cascade.

"Twenty dollars," said Madame, lifting the mass.

"Give it to me quick," said Della.

The next two hours tripped by on rosy wings. Della was ransacking the stores to find Jim's present. She found it at last. It surely had been made for Jim and no one else. There was no other like it in any of the stores. It was a fob chain, simple in design, properly proclaiming its value by substance alone. As soon as she saw it she knew that it must be Jim's. It was like him. Quietness and value applied to both. Twenty-one dollars they took from her for it, and she hurried home with the change.

With that chain on his watch Jim might be properly anxious about the time in any company.

When Della reached home her intoxication gave way a little to prudence and reason. She got out her curling iron and went to work repairing the ravages made by generosity and love.

Within forty minutes her head was covered with tiny, close-lying curls that made her look a bit like a truant schoolboy. She looked at her reflection in the mirror long and carefully.

"If Jim doesn't kill me," she said to herself, "he'll say I look like a Coney Island chorus girl. But what could I do? Oh! what could I do with a dollar and eighty-seven cents?"

At seven o'clock the coffee was made and the frying pan was sitting on the back of the stove. It was hot and ready to cook the pork chops that Della had bought the night before. Jim was never late. Della doubled the fob chain in her hand and sat on the corner of the table nearest the door.

Then Della heard Jim's step on the stairs way down on the first flight. Quickly, she stood up and fixed her hair one last time. Then she turned white for just a moment.

Della had a habit of saying little prayers about the simplest everyday things, and now she whispered, "Please God, make him think I am still pretty."

The door opened and Jim stepped in. He looked very serious. Poor fellow, he was only twenty-two and already burdened with a family! He needed a new coat, and he was without gloves.

"Hello dear," Jim said. Then he looked up at Della. His eyes were fixed upon Della as she stood there.

Della tried to smile, until she looked into his eyes. There was an expression in them that she could not read. It was not anger, nor surprise, nor disapproval, nor any of the sentiments that she had been prepared for.

Jim simply stared at her fixedly with that peculiar expression on his face.

Della finally reached out her hand. "Jim, darling," she cried, "please don't look at me that way. I had my hair cut off and sold because I could not have lived through Christmas without giving you a real present. And I certainly didn't have enough money saved to buy a present."

Della looked into Jim's eyes. "It will grow out again," she said. "You won't mind, will you? I just had to do it. My hair grows awfully fast. Please say 'Merry Christmas!' Jim, and let's be happy."

"You've cut off your hair?" asked Jim, as if he had not arrived at that patent fact yet even after the hardest mental labor.

Della held his hand tighter still, warming it with her own. "Cut it off and sold it," said Della. "Don't you like me just as well, anyhow? I'm me without my hair. Don't you think so?"

Jim looked about the room curiously. "You say your hair is gone?" he said, with an air of idiocy.

"You needn't look for it," said Della. "It's sold, I tell you, sold and gone, too. Be good to me, for it went for you. Maybe the hairs of my head were numbered," she went on with a sudden sweetness, "but nobody could ever count my love for you."

Della waited for Jim to speak then. He took off his coat without speaking and then turned back to her.

Out of his trance Jim seemed quickly to wake. He grabbed Della in his arms.

For a few seconds let us regard with discreet scrutiny some inconsequential object in the other direction. Eight dollars a week or a million a year, what is the difference? A mathematician would give you the wrong answer. The Magi brought some very valuable gifts, but that was not among them. This dark assertion will be illuminated later on.

Jim drew a package from his overcoat pocket and threw it upon the table. "Make no mistake, Dell, about me," he said. "I don't think there is anything in the way of a haircut that could make me like my girl any less. But if you will unwrap that package you may see why you had me going awhile at first."

White, nimble fingers tore at the string and paper. Della let out an ecstatic scream of joy.

Then her voice turned to hysterical tears and wails as she examined the contents of the box.

For there lay "the combs."

They were the combs that Della had worshiped in a Broadway window. Beautiful combs with jeweled rims, just the shade to wear in the beautiful vanished hair. They were very expensive combs, and her heart had simply yearned for them without the least hope of possession. And now, they were hers, but the long tresses that should have adorned them were gone.

Jim said, "I can take the combs back and get the money instead."

But Della just hugged them to her bosom. "My hair grows so fast, Jim!" she cried. "I'll be able to use them in a few months."

"Then you should keep them," said Jim. "They will look beautiful in your hair."

And then Della leaped up and cried, "Oh, oh!" Jim had not yet seen his beautiful present. She held it out to him eagerly upon her open palm. The dull precious metal seemed to flash with a reflection of her bright and ardent spirit.

"Isn't it a dandy, Jim?" Della asked. "I hunted all over town to find it. Give me your watch. I want to see how it looks on it."

Instead of obeying, Jim tumbled down on the couch and put his hands under the back of his head and smiled.

"Dell," said Jim, "let's put our Christmas presents away and keep them awhile. They're too nice to use just yet. I sold the watch to get the money to buy your combs. And now suppose we get dinner ready."

The Magi, as you know, were wise men who brought gifts to the babe in the manger.

These Wise Men invented the art of giving Christmas presents. And here I have related to you the uneventful chronicle of two foolish children in a flat who most unwisely sacrificed for each other the greatest treasures of their house.

But in a last word to the wise of these days let it be said that of all who give gifts these two were the wisest. Of all who give and receive gifts, they are wisest.

They are the Magi.

Christmas Songs

God Rest Ye Merry Gentlemen

London

Vigorously

1. God rest ye merry gentlemen, Let nothing ye dismay. Remember Christ our Saviour was born on Christmas day. To
2. From God our heav'nly father, A blessed Angel came, And unto certain shepherds brought tidings of the same. How

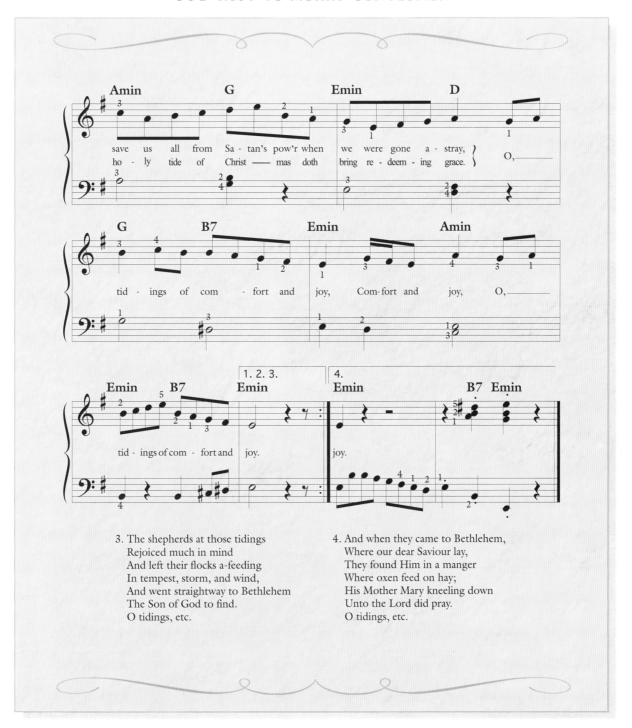

3. The shepherds at those tidings
Rejoiced much in mind
And left their flocks a-feeding
In tempest, storm, and wind,
And went straightway to Bethlehem
The Son of God to find.
O tidings, etc.

4. And when they came to Bethlehem,
Where our dear Saviour lay,
They found Him in a manger
Where oxen feed on hay;
His Mother Mary kneeling down
Unto the Lord did pray.
O tidings, etc.

Here We Come A-Caroling

England

Lively

C

1. Here we come a-car-ol-ing, A-mong the leaves so
2. Our was-sail cup is made of the rose - ma - ry

green, Here we come a-wan-der-ing so
tree, And so is your beer of the

F **C** **G7**

3. We are not daily beggars
   That beg from door to door,
   But we are neighbors' children
   Whom you have seen before.
   Love and joy, etc.

4. God bless the master of this house,
   Likewise the mistress too,
   And all the little children
   That round the table go.
   Love and joy, etc.

O Christmas Tree

2. O Christmas tree, O Christmas tree,
   Much pleasure doth thou bring me.
   For every year the Christmas tree,
   Brings to us all both joy and glee.
   O Christmas tree, O Christmas tree,
   Much pleasure doth thou bring me.

3. O Christmas tree, O Christmas tree,
   Thy candles shine out brightly.
   Each bough doth hold its tiny light,
   That makes each toy to sparkle bright.
   O Christmas tree, O Christmas tree,
   Thy candles shine out brightly.

O Little Town of Bethlehem

Reverently

1.O lit - tle town of Beth - le - hem, How still we— see thee lie. A-

bove thy deep and dream- less sleep, The si - lent— stars go by. Yet

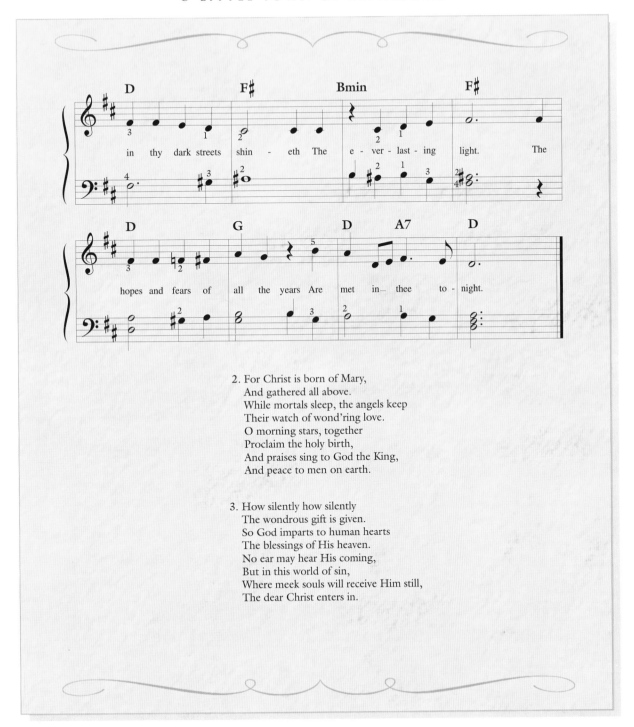

2. For Christ is born of Mary,
   And gathered all above.
   While mortals sleep, the angels keep
   Their watch of wond'ring love.
   O morning stars, together
   Proclaim the holy birth,
   And praises sing to God the King,
   And peace to men on earth.

3. How silently how silently
   The wondrous gift is given.
   So God imparts to human hearts
   The blessings of His heaven.
   No ear may hear His coming,
   But in this world of sin,
   Where meek souls will receive Him still,
   The dear Christ enters in.

While Shepherds Watched Their Flocks

George Frederick Handel

While shep-herds watched their flocks by night, All seat-ed on the ground, The an-gel of the Lord came down, And

glo - ry shone a - round,_____ And glo - ry shone a - round.

2. "Fear not," said he; for mighty dread
   Had seized their trouble mind;
   "Glad tidings of great joy I bring
   To you and all mankind."

3. "To you in David's town this day
   Is born of David's line
   A Savior, who is Christ the Lord;
   And this shall be the sign."

4. "The heavenly Babe you there shall find
   To human view displayed,
   All meanly wrapped in swathing bands,
   And in a manger laid."

5. Thus spake the seraph; and forthwith
   Appeared a shining throng
   Of angels praising God, who thus
   Addressed their joyful song.

6. "All glory be to God on high,
   And to the earth be peace;
   Good-will henceforth from heaven to men
   Begin and never cease."

O Come All Ye Faithful

Latin: J. Reading
English translation: Rev. F. Oakeley

Traditional

Majestically

mf 1.O come, all ye faith - ful, joy - ful and tri - um - phant, O

come ye, O come ye to Beth - le - hem.

2. Sing, choirs of angels, sing in exultation,
Sing, all ye citizens of heav'n above.
Glory to God, all glory in the highest,
O come, etc.

3. Yea Lord, we greet Thee, born this happy morning,
Jesus, to Thee be glory giv'n.
Word of the Father, now in flesh appearing.
O come, etc.

Joy to the World

Words: Isaac Watts

Music: George F. Handel

1. Joy to the world, The Lord is come, Let

earth re - ceive her King, Let

2. Joy to the world, the Savior reigns,
   Let men their songs employ,
   While fields and floods,
   Rocks, hills, and plains,
   Repeat the sounding joy,
   Repeat the sounding joy,
   Repeat, repeat the sounding joy.

3. He rules the world with truth and grace,
   And makes the nations prove,
   The glories of
   His righteousness,
   And wonders of His love,
   And wonders of His love,
   And wonders, wonders of His love.

Hark! The Herald Angels Sing

Words: Charles Wesley

Music: Felix Mendelssohn

2. Christ by highest heav'n adored,
   Christ the everlasting Lord!
   Late in time behold Him come,
   Offspring of a virgin's womb.
   Veiled in flesh the Godhead see,
   Hail the Incarnate Deity,
   Pleased with men as man to dwell,
   Jesus our Immanuel!
   Hark! The herald angels sing
   Glory to the newborn King.

3. Hail, the heav'n-born Prince of Peace!
   Hail, the Son of Righteousness!
   Life and light to all He brings,
   Ris'n with healing in His wings.
   Mild He lays His glory by,
   Born that man no more may die,
   Born to raise the sons of earth,
   Born to give them second birth.
   Hark! The herald angels sing
   Glory to the newborn King.

Away in a Manger

Old Lutheran Carol

2. The cattle are lowing, the Baby awakes
   But little Lord Jesus, no crying He makes.
   I love Thee, Lord Jesus, look down from the sky,
   And stay by my cradle till morning is nigh.

3. Be near me, Lord Jesus, I ask Thee to stay
   Close by me forever, and love me, I pray.
   Bless all the dear children in Thy tender care,
   And fit us to Heaven to live with Thee there.

Silent Night

Fr. Joseph Mohr
Franz Gruber

1.Si - lent night, Ho - ly night! All is calm, all is bright. Round yon Vir - gin Moth - er and

2. Silent night, Holy night!
   Shepherds quake at the sight.
   Glories stream from heaven afar,
   Heav'nly hosts sing Hallelujah,
   Christ the Saviour is born,
   Christ the Saviour is born.

3. Silent night, Holy night!
   Son of God, love's pure light.
   Radiant beams from Thy holy face,
   With the dawn of redeeming grace,
   Jesus Lord at Thy birth,
   Jesus Lord at Thy birth.

The First Noel

Old English

2. They looked up and saw a star
   Shining in the East beyond them far,
   And to the earth it gave great light,
   And so it continued both day and night.
   Noel, etc.

3. This star drew nigh to the northwest,
   O'er Bethlehem it took its rest.
   And there it did both stop and stay
   Right over the place where Jesus lay.
   Noel, etc.

We Three Kings

John H. Hopkins

The Twelve Days of Christmas

Traditional

1.On the first day of Christ-mas my true love gave to me: A par-tridge— in a pear tree. 2.On the sec-ond day of Christ-mas my

Jolly Old St. Nicholas

American

With a bounce

1.Jol - ly old Saint Nich - o - las, Lean your ear this way,

Don't you tell a sin - gle soul What I'm going to say.

2. When the clock is striking twelve,
   When I'm fast asleep.
   Down the chimney broad and black,
   With your pack you'll creep.

   All the stockings you will find
   Hanging in a row.
   Mine will be the shortest one
   You'll be sure to know.

3. Johnny wants a pair of skates.
   Susy wants a sled.
   Nellie wants a picture book,
   Yellow, blue and red.

   Now I think I'll leave to you
   What to give the rest.
   Choose for me, dear Santa Claus,
   You will know the best.

Up on the house-top click, click, click, Down through the chim-ney with good Saint Nick.

2. First comes the stocking of little Nell;
   Oh, dear Santa fill it well;
   Give her a dollie that laughs and cries
   One that will open and shut her eyes.

3. Next comes the stocking of little Will;
   Oh, just see what a glorious fill!
   Here is a hammer and plastic tacks,
   Also a ball and a game of jacks.

Jingle Bells

J. Pierpont

Dance of the Sugar Plum Fairy

Rhythmically and Delicately
2nd time play both hands one octave higher

Tchaikovsky
from *The Nutcracker Suite*

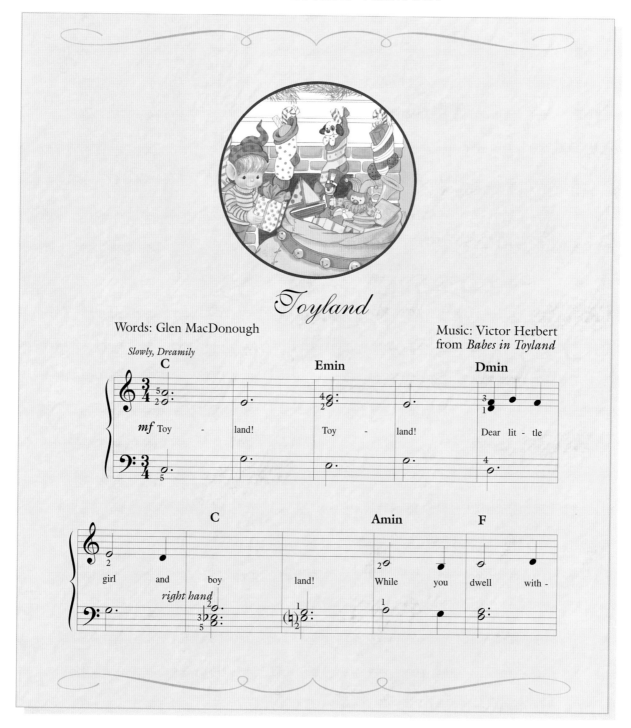

Toyland

Words: Glen MacDonough

Music: Victor Herbert
from *Babes in Toyland*

Slowly, Dreamily

mf Toy - land! Toy - land! Dear lit - tle girl and boy land! While you dwell with -

Deck the Halls

Welsh

Don we now our gay ap-par-el, Fa la la la la la la la la,

Troll the an-cient yule-tide car-ol, Fa la la la la la la la la.

2. See the blazing yule before us,
   Fa la, etc.
   Strike the harp and join the chorus,
   Fa la, etc.
   Follow me in merry measure,
   Fa la, etc.
   While I tell of Christmas treasure.
   Fa la, etc.

3. Fast away the old year passes,
   Fa la, etc.
   Hail the new! ye lads and lasses;
   Fa la, etc.
   Sing we joyous all together,
   Fa la, etc.
   Heedless of the wind and weather.
   Fa la, etc.

I Saw Three Ships

England

1.I saw three ships come sail - ing in, On

Christ - mas Day, On Christ - mas Day, I

2. And what was in those ships all three,
   On Christmas Day, On Christmas Day?
   And what was in those ships all three,
   On Christmas Day in the morning?

3. The Virgin Mary and Christ were there,
   On Christmas Day, On Christmas Day,
   The Virgin Mary and Christ were there,
   On Christmas Day in the morning.

O Holy Night

Adolphe Adam

Reverently

O ho - ly night,——— the stars are bright - ly shin - ing, This is the night of our dear Sav - ior's birth. Long lay the world——— in sin and er - ror

Good tid - ings we bring to you and your kin, Good
tid - ings for Christ - mas and a hap - py New Year.

2. Now bring us some figgy pudding,
   Now bring us some figgy pudding,
   Now bring us some figgy pudding
   And a cup of good cheer!

3. We won't go until we get some,
   We won't go until we get some,
   We won't go until we get some,
   So bring it out here.

Angels We Have Heard on High

Traditional

In ex - cel - sis De - o, De - o

2. Shepards, why this jubilee?
   Why your joyous strains prolong?
   What the gladsome tidings be
   Which inspire your heav'nly song?
   Gloria, etc.

3. Come to Bethlehem and see
   Him whose birth the angels sing;
   Come, adore on bended knee
   Christ the Lord, the newborn King.
   Gloria, etc.

4. See him in a manger laid
   Whom the angels praise above.
   Mary, Joseph, lend your aid,
   While we raise our hearts in love.
   Gloria, etc.

It Came Upon a Midnight Clear

Words: Edmund Sears

Music: Richard Willis

1. It came up-on a mid-night clear, that glo-rious song of old, From an-gels bend-ing near the earth, To touch their harps of

Merry Christmas!